Nula

Frank J Gratton

Nula

Olympia Publishers
London

www.olympiapublishers.com

OLYMPIA PAPERBACK EDITION

A CIP catalogue record for this title is
available from the British Library.

ISBN: 978-1-80074-276-5

First Published in 2022

Olympia Publishers
Tallis House
2 Tallis Street
London
EC4Y 0AB

Printed in Great Britain

Dedication

To all those who gaze into the night sky and dare to believe.

Chapter One

Farmhouse at Kensey International, Schuylerville, New York

Frank slowly slid himself out of bed so that he would not wake his wife, Marian. He was careful not to step on the squeaky floorboard as he had done so many times before. He looked down at her. Even while sleeping, she was an astonishingly beautiful woman. *My miracle girl*, he thought. The dim light glowed on her long black hair partially covering her face, hiding her full beauty. He softly pushed her locks back with two fingers. What a fortunate man he was to have this magnificent woman in his life. He had almost lost her once but had been blessed with a second chance.

He moved slowly to the bathroom, thinking that the old farmhouse always surprised him with new squeaks and groans. He stood in front of the mirror and raised his razor to his face. He stopped. The reflection showed an aging man. His once shiny black hair was now peppered with grey and his sideburns were totally grey. His physique had lost much of its definition. He was still thin with handsome features, but he knew that much of his strength was gone. He had once owned and operated a twenty-five-hundred-acre dairy farm that demanded much physical labor, and he had been a sturdy, brawny man back then. That ended eight years ago. He had thought about closing the farm down, but he could not live with himself knowing he would have to lay off all the dedicated workers who had become like family over the years. He had decreased the farm to two hundred acres and given it to the workers.

He finished in the bathroom, threw the towel in the hamper, moved to the door, then turned and took the hamper. He didn't want his wife to have to carry it down the stairs. He had started doing small insignificant tasks for her right after the miracle. He closed the door to their bedroom so gently that you could hardly hear the slight click. The doors to Kevin's and Theresa's rooms were open, as usual, they were empty. He knew they were both already on Broken Bone Hill. For the past six years, they were up before sunrise and working on their project before breakfast. He still felt chills run through him and could recall the terror on his wife's face when they had explained what they were building. He had talked to his wife for hours about it, and they had decided that their idea was so far-fetched that it would never happen, so why worry. But it troubled him. After all, Kevin was a child prodigy, at least that's what the board of directors called him.

Hamper under his arm, he tried to navigate the stairs without making a sound, but it was impossible. As he descended, each step groaned dissatisfaction with its own unique squeak. At the bottom, he turned left down a short hallway leading to the laundry room. He placed the hamper on the dryer. The room was immaculate. The shelves were freshly painted with white enamel and every item was neatly labeled and placed on shelves. Kevin had taken it upon himself to lay out every room in the house this way so that his mom would have little or no work to do. Theresa soon caught on to what he was doing and eagerly helped.

Frank separated the laundry but did not turn on the

washing machine. He walked to the kitchen, took the coffee pot and began filling it with water while looking out the window over the sink. He placed the full pot on the counter. He could see that the farm workers were already well into their chores. He missed it so much that he had begun rising at four thirty a.m. to have breakfast before going down to the barns to help. He wanted no pay, just the work and the camaraderie. He had worked, celebrated and cried with these folks for over twenty years. He usually stayed at the dairy farm till nine a.m. and then headed over to one of the twelve huge warehouse type buildings that had been constructed on a one-thousand-acre parcel a good distance away from the barns. Once there, he would oversee three hundred or so employees. He was never quite sure of the number because Kevin or Theresa were always hiring, transferring or dismissing personnel.

It was now going on five a.m. and Frank had hoped that Kevin and Theresa would meet him for breakfast. He scrambled extra eggs just in case. He toasted a couple of extra slices of home-made bread and smothered them with fresh butter. He gulped down a mouthful of milk and sat alone at the table, deep in thought.

A slight knock at the back door brought him out of his trance. He knew it would be Al. He finished his milk and went to the door. A warm spring breeze flooded the kitchen along with the aroma of fresh flowers that his wife had planted a few days earlier.

"Morning, Al. That alarm acting up again?" Frank asked.

"I'm sorry, Frank. I know it's a false reading but I've got to check it out." Al shook his head. "The technicians have been working on it all week. Just can't figure it out."

"Come on in and join me. I made it strong this morning,"

Frank said, holding up the freshly brewed pot of coffee he had grabbed off the stove next to the door.

"No, thanks. I know you want to get to the barns."

"Have you seen the kids?" Frank asked.

"No, but Jim in surveillance had them on camera going to the hill. They started early today."

"How early?" Frank looked up, surprised.

"Two a.m.. Jim told me they were waiting for a delivery. Three trucks arrived at 2:19 a.m."

"Kind of early for a delivery. What was in the trucks?" Frank said, moving to the table.

"Don't know. I'll call the gate and have them text me the invoices," Al said, retrieving his phone from his back pocket.

Al was already on his phone as he stepped into the kitchen. Frank placed a cup of black coffee on the table and motioned for Al to sit. Over the years, they had shared many navy stories over a cup of strong brew. Al called it boatswain's mate coffee on a warm day and Mississippi mud on a winter's day.

Al read the message, shook his head and handed his phone to Frank. "You know what that stuff is?"

Frank looked at the items displayed on the delivery statements. "Nope, can't say that I do."

Frank spoke into his phone. "What is graphene?"

Graphene is a two-dimensional crystalline structure of carbon, one hundred times stronger than steel but ninety per cent lighter, the device replied.

"I tell you, Boss, I learn something new every day that I work here," Al said, shaking his head.

Frank asked the phone, "What are graphite carbon nanotubes?" The phone burst forth with four pages of information. He sat quietly while he read slowly. "There's a lot of information here, Al, but to keep it short, the nanotubes can be roped together to form an ultra-high strength, low weight material."

"Got to be something they need for that thing they're building up on the hill. It gets bigger every day. Did the kids let you in on the big secret yet?" Al asked, blowing over his coffee mug.

Frank took a sip of his coffee, gazing into the bottom of the cup. He looked up and handed the phone to Al.

"Sorry, Boss. I should know better. It's just that yesterday morning Kevin hired twenty more security guards. Not for nothing, but these guys looked like ex-military." Al pushed up from the table and headed for the door. "Thanks for the coffee, Boss. Oh, by the way, look at the last invoice." He held the phone up so Frank could read, *Twenty cases of cola.*

"What the heck?" Frank said softly. They stood staring at each other for a moment before Al broke the silence.

"One more thing. Theresa put the hill on a total lockdown at four this morning. It was strange because she came to the surveillance room and ordered a sweep of Building Thirteen and, when that was called in as all clear, she shut off and coded the cameras, then ordered all security off the hill. Said she would be in later to turn them back on."

Frank froze. *Must be getting close,* he thought, a sick wheezy feeling coming over him. He willed himself to calm down. "Has she been back in to turn them on?" Frank said, struggling to make his voice sound normal.

"Not yet," Al said, already halfway down the steps.

"Text me when she comes into surveillance." Frank was thinking about driving up to the hill but knew that security would follow Kevin's orders and not allow anyone into the area.

"Will do, Boss. I'll be in touch," Al yelled from his golf cart while driving away.

Looks like that far-fetched idea was about to happen. Frank filled his cup with the hot boatswain's mate brew, moved to the table and collapsed onto the chair. With elbows on the table and hands to his forehead, he chided himself for allowing this to go this far. His mind began racing through the past nine years. He immediately became emotional. He wiped the tears from his eyes as he thought of his wife laying in the hospital bed nine years ago, totally broken and disfigured from a horrific car collision. The doctor had declared her brain dead. He relived the tremendous hopelessness he had felt; a sob escaped as the pain of losing her felt as real and alive as if it were happening at that moment. The call had come early one Friday morning. That awful, cold-hearted person telling him that his wife was barely alive and that he should get there right away.

He recalled that one day when he was going to visit her, Kevin had asked to go with him. Why he had allowed Kevin and his new friend, Billbet, to go to the hospital was still a mystery. He had promised himself that he would never allow the children to see their mom broken and battered. He'd wanted them to remember her as the beautiful women she once was. He just hadn't been thinking clearly. He had told the two boys to stay in the lobby but, once he left them, they'd both gone to the intensive care unit. Kevin had pleaded with the nurse to let him see his mom, but she'd adamantly refused until Marian's doctor had intervened. Not knowing Frank's desire about the children's visits, he'd instructed the nurse to allow them into Marian's room.

Then came the commotion. The entire ward was in total confusion. Nurses running about from room to room. Visitors crying, some laughing, others yelling. Patients began sitting up and others got out of bed while nurses attempted to make them lie down.

Before this mayhem, Frank had been standing behind the curtain to his wife's room with both hands covering his mouth, trying desperately to muffle his sobbing. Then, as if watching a flower blooming in slow motion, her smashed blackened eyes began to clear, her broken jaw formed a smile. Sobs exploded through his clasped hands. When she opened those gorgeous brown eyes, he fell to his knees.

During all this commotion, no one had noticed Kevin's friend, Billbet, slightly touching each patient on the ward. He went from room to room and when finished stood silently next to Kevin.

There were whispers throughout the intensive care unit that all the patients were somehow healed. The doctors were unwilling to use the word miracle but when Marian's doctor was finally able to talk to Frank in private, he broke down and, with tears streaming down his face, admitted that there had been multiple miracles.

Two months after that event, Kevin went to his parents and explained what had really happened. He told them that his friend, Billbet, had healed everyone. That his new friend was from a planet called Ursa and that he had landed on Earth and was completely lost. At first, they'd both laughed with delight, relishing the imagination of a ten year old. But he had insisted that they go with him to Broken Bone Hill. He wanted to show them the downed trees, the scorched earth, the marks embedded in the ground from where Billbet's spacecraft landed. He brought them to each indentation, counting as he went. When he came to number twelve, he stopped and looked up at them, tears filling his eyes. Frank stared at his wife and they both smiled. Kevin knew he had not convinced them, so he showed them the glow star. He said it was given to him by Billbet's dad as a gift for helping Billbet get back home. The object was small, but it glowed so brightly in the palm of his hand that it seemed it should be extremely hot. His parents touched it but felt nothing.

Frank broke through his trance. He reached in his back pocket and retrieved his cell phone. He spoke to it. "Dial surveillance."

"Surveillance. This is Jim. Good morning, Mister Kensey."

"Morning, Jim. Any word from Kevin or Theresa?" Frank asked, nervously fidgeting with his coffee cup.

"Not yet, Mister Kensey."

"Does T still have you on lockdown?"

"Theresa did not totally lock us down, sir, just Building Thirteen."

"OK. Thanks, Jim. Do you have any idea who's in the building?"

"Just Kevin and Theresa, sir. They put twelve security guards around the perimeter with instructions not to allow anyone through the gate."

"Can you check the electrical input to that location and let me know if there were any dramatic increases in power demand?" Frank asked, hoping to get a clue as to what the kids were up to.

"Sure. I'll put you on hold for a second." Jim rolled his

chair over to the command station and pressed the radio transmission button. "Surveillance to engineering."

"Engineering on," the response came immediately.

"Are you sitting on the mic," Jim said jokingly.

"What's up, Jim?" Eugene asked from the other end.

"Got Mister Kensey on hold. He wants you to check for any unusual power demand from Building Thirteen."

"One second," Eugene responded as he punched the request into his computer. "Nope. Power's been stable. Nothing going on in that ugly monstrosity," he said.

"You better not let the boss hear you talk like that," Jim scolded.

"Come on, Jim, you got to admit—"

"Stop!" Jim demanded, interrupting Eugene before he could finish. "For what they pay you, you should keep your thoughts to yourself." He ended the transmission, thinking of how Kensey employees were the best paid on the globe.

"Sorry for the wait, Mister Kensey. Engineering reports that power consumption is normal. Is everything OK, sir?"

"Everything is fine, Jim. Just haven't heard from the kids this morning," Frank answered, trying to hide the concern in his voice.

"I'll text you as soon as I hear from one of them. You know how Kevin is when he's working on one of his projects."

"That would be great if you could keep me informed. But I expect I'll hear from them soon." Frank knew what Jim was implying was true. But his fear was that Kevin and Theresa were in the final stage of their plan. He dismissed this assumption, knowing that the kids would not go any further without first speaking to him and their mother.

Frank decided not to go to the dairy farm. Instead, he

instructed his phone to dial Kevin. His mind tuned out the ringing; he thought back to the night he was on his way to bed and, as he walked past Kevin's room at two in the morning, he noticed Kevin and Theresa huddled around Kevin's desk. The only sound was Kevin's frantic typing on the computer keyboard, as if he was possessed or in some altered state or trance. Theresa was sitting next to him with her eyes closed, her left hand on Kevin's shoulder. Frank stood quietly in the hallway and waited for Kevin to stop typing but, after what seemed like an eternity, he broke the silence. "What are you two up to?" he whispered.

Theresa quickly pulled her hand off Kevin's shoulder as if she had been caught in some indecent act. "Ahhh, nothing, Dad," she said, her face red from the lie.

Kevin had his left hand raised in the air with his index finger up indicating that he wanted to finish the thought he was typing. A few moments later he swiveled in his chair, took a hard look at his dad and said, "You're up late, Dad."

"What's going on?" Frank asked in a louder and sterner voice.

"I'm talking to Billbet. Well, not actually talking, more like a video," Kevin said calmly, as if this was as normal as watching TV.

"Stop this nonsense, Kevin," Frank demanded, walking into the room and looking over Kevin's shoulder. He read the two sentences on the screen. *Before you ignite the thrusters be sure the helium indicator light is yellow. This will assure that the system has been purged of any air bubbles in the fuel lines.* Frank stood over the screen until Kevin broke the silence.

"Dad." Kevin tried to explain.

Frank cut him off. "It's two in the morning and you're

talking foolishness."

"But, Dad, Billbet needs—" Theresa said, but Frank cut her off too.

"Please, T, go to bed now. We'll talk in the morning," Frank said quietly. "I don't want to wake your mother."

"Dad, we can't. Billbet is in training and Theresa and I are in class with him. I know this sounds unbelievable but it's as if we are in the same room with him. It's not my imagination. It's real and extremely important." Kevin looked at his dad with pleading eyes.

"Kevin, you're only eleven. You have school in the morning and that's what is important."

"We're at school now," Kevin said, his right hand outstretched and holding the glow star, its brilliant light filling the room. "Put your hand over the glow, Dad. It's as if it's coaching me on what to do next. I have these wild ideas that flood my mind and somehow the solutions and instructions of how to create them and make them a reality pop into my mind. I tried at first to ignore them, but there is a force convincing me to act. It's not a frightening feeling but a soothing calmness."

Kevin had shown the star to him and Marian on Broken Bone Hill but had given no explanation as to what it was. Frank moved slowly towards the glow and held his hand over his son's. Before, on the hill, he had felt nothing from the glow star but now it radiated a soothing warmth. A contented, calm feeling filled his entire being. His mind was instructing him to trust what his son was saying. The nagging, frightening emotions he was feeling dissolved. It was only after Kevin lowered his hand and put the glow star on his desk that his dad put his hand down, breaking the spell.

"How are you talking to Billbet? Where's your phone? Where's Billbet?" Frank asked rapidly.

The room went silent for a moment. Kevin looked at Theresa and said softly, "He'll never understand."

"Understand what?" Frank said, speaking louder than he wanted to.

Kevin stood up and opened his closet door. Theresa and Frank followed. Displayed on the back of the door were maps of the planets and stars in the universe. Kevin pointed to the furthest dot on the map and said, "He's here."

Frank had squinted to read the word Thessus and dropped his shoulder in despair. "Don't you know how ridiculous that sounds?" he'd asked.

Frank was jolted back to reality when his phone squawked, *Please leave a message after the tone.* No answer from Kevin. He disconnected.

He remembered how he had stormed out of Kevin's room frustrated that his son and daughter were wasting their time on such foolish games that late on a school night. He recalled how he could not get the word Thessus out of his head. The next day he went to the library and wasted an hour trying to find information on a planet or moon named Thessus. Nothing! Kevin had made that up, he thought. What a fool I am. He would soon be proven wrong.

Everything moved rapidly after that night's encounter with Kevin. Within six months, Kevin had designed, developed and patented a new computer microdot, capable of storing hundreds of times more information than anything currently available. With the sale of the patent, Kevin dropped out of school and Kensey International was created. Theresa left school the following year and assisted her brother with inventing hundreds of new products. Billions of dollars poured into the corporation. Kevin had told the family that he could not use any of the money for his personal gratification. No fancy cars, or extravagant homes. No vacations, not even a night out on the town. The glow star would only reveal its secrets to someone with the purest of intentions. Most of the profits went to the employees, making them the best paid people on earth. Once the word got out about their generous benefit package, Kensey International had no trouble attracting the brightest people worldwide.

Of course, some money was going to Kevin and Theresa's top secret project. The world had labeled him a child genius, a visionary, but he explained to his parents that he was none of these things. He explained that the glow star was instructing him step-by-step. His intentions needed to be completely pure for him to experience any solution to what he imagined. The only ideas that could be created were those that benefitted the population of the universe.

Frank remembered that they'd soon understand the frightening reality to his alluding to the universe.

Chapter Two

"So much blood!" Theresa said as she moved the suction tube back and forth to remove the flowing blood from where Dauntless's thumb had once been. She was wearing a surgical mask and rubber apron. Her long black hair was stuffed into a white cap that resembled a large bowl. A bright light emanated from the LED mirror strapped to her head, illuminating Dauntless's hand. His amputated thumb was in a bowl of alcohol. "Why doesn't it hurt?"

Dauntless and his sister's eyes met. *God, she has mom's eyes.* It was obvious now that they were the only facial features he could see. *No wonder people get them confused.* "I told you that the new gas would work. We tested it enough," Dauntless responded. His left hand was strapped to a small platform inside a sealed operating compartment filled with the invisible painkilling gas.

"Oh, you're so dang smart," Theresa said jokingly. "You better be nice, Kevin." She held the scalpel up menacingly in her left hand. Both her hands were inserted in surgical gloves that were attached to the clear glass compartment, ensuring no outside contaminants would affect the operation.

"Dauntless! It's Dauntless," he corrected. "Pay attention. Just that one nerve left." He used a needle pointer to draw attention to a strand the size of a tiny thread. He pushed a large magnifying light closer with the back of his free hand. Theresa took her time and, with precision, made the difficult connection. "Perfect." He placed the pointer on the tray and opened the incubator next to the operating compartment and retrieved the bionic thumb. It was exactly like the original except for the movable fingernail. He would be able to open and close the nail with a slight flick of the new device.

"Why can't I have a new name? I graduated same as you," Theresa pouted.

"My God! Can't we talk about this later?" Dauntless said, slightly annoyed.

"Kevin. Oh, sorry Dauntlesssss," Theresa answered with a sarcastic tone. "I can finish with my eyes closed. God knows we practiced on the clone hand enough times."

It took Theresa two hours to attach the bionic thumb. Dauntless tried to correct her a number of times but kept apologizing after she gave him a look with those big brown eyes as if to say, "Really?" She applied a generous amount of the healing lotion that Dauntless had developed, then stepped away to admire her work. Dauntless was wiggling the new thumb and flicking it, opening and closing the secret compartment. When he was pleased with its functioning abilities, he removed the glow star from the incubator, placed it into the compartment and, with a flick, hid it with his new thumbnail. Theresa had removed her surgical clothing and was standing over the operating table and smiling, her head tilted to one side.

Dauntless gave her a long, strong hug. "I love you, T."

"Love you also." Then she whispered in his ear, "I want a new name." She removed herself from the hug. "You're now

Dauntless, Billbet is Stone. It's only fair," she continued as they both began the clean-up of the operation room.

"OK. OK," Dauntless agreed, throwing the trash in the fireless disposal receptacle. "It's just that I'm the only one who knows you were in the cadet class. Can't get a name if no one knows you're there," Dauntless said, attempting to explain but realizing it was useless. "I promise when we get there, I'll talk to Stone."

"After all these years, I would have thought you'd at least mentioned me," Theresa said as they left the operating room and were on their way to the flight deck. "You know Mom and Dad are never going to call you Dauntless."

"Oh, how about Annoying? That seems to describe you," Dauntless countered.

Theresa punched him softly in the arm. "A child genius," she said, making imaginary quotation marks in the air with her fingers, "would be more creative."

They entered the flight deck and stood in front of Prodigy, the self-learning quantum supercomputer. Five years ago, Dauntless and Theresa, guided by the glow star, had mastered the singularity technology which allowed Prodigy's components to greatly surpass human performance. It took another year for them to develop the computer chips that would prevent Prodigy's growth from becoming uncontrollable and irreversible, resulting in unforeseeable change to human civilization.

Prodigy recognized them as they entered the room. "Your dad has been trying to reach you," the computer instructed.

"What time is it, Prodigy?" Dauntless asked as he walked over to the bank of monitors. He was wiggling his new thumb. *No pain and it felt just like the old one.* He punched in Bseventy-four through B-one-zero-two onto the keyboard. Instantly the monitors displayed the cameras located in the three-dimensional printer room. There were so many that a number of monitors had to display the cameras' images onto split screens.

"Please be specific," Prodigy requested.

"Real time, New York State, United States of America," Dauntless shot back.

"Eight forty-five and twenty seconds and counting," Prodigy responded.

"T, you call surveillance and give them the code to bring their camera system back online. I'll call Dad."

Dauntless speed dialed his dad.

"Good morning, Kevin. Everything all right?" Frank asked.

"We did that thumb thing this morning," Dauntless said, not wanting to correct his dad for not using his new name.

"How did it go?"

"Perfect, Dad. Give us a half hour and we'll meet you at the house," Dauntless said while scanning the three-dimensional printer room.

"OK. Mom will be up by then. You two want breakfast?"

"Absolutely. See you then. Got to go, Dad." Dauntless clicked off to end the transmission.

Dauntless turned in his chair and overheard his sister say, "Prodigy, give me another name based on my strongest character." He shook his head, smiling.

"Beautiful," Prodigy instantly answered.

"Flattery will get you everywhere," she said, blowing a kiss to Prodigy.

"Prodigy, report on the bees," Dauntless said, swinging his chair around so he could see the monitors displaying the cameras in the three-dimensional printer room.

"Ten are finished, and the three-dimensional printers are in the final stages of another two. One of the diamonds split during the infusion process and needed to be replaced. All other atomic diamond batteries were successfully installed and the ten completed bees are programed to my files and are fully operational," Prodigy responded.

"Let's take one home," Theresa said, looking at Dauntless with a huge grin. "Mom and Dad will be so surprised."

Dauntless remained silent. He was thinking about the repercussions that might cause. Theresa never took her eyes off him. She shrugged her shoulders and held her palms up. "Well! Derr!"

Dauntless had programed a few surprise capabilities for the bees. The one that concerned him the most was the powerful laser stinger. "Prodigy, program PB One to Theresa's DNA. Disable laser. Authorize Theresa full capabilities on her command." He turned towards his sister and raised his eyebrows. "Done. Prodigy Bee One is yours."

"Laser! Really!" Theresa said.

"You never know. Call your bee."

"PB One, come to my location," Theresa commanded.

It took a few minutes for PB One to navigate the hallways but, when it arrived at the command center, it followed protocol and requested, "Permission to enter."

Theresa gave Dauntless a hard stare. "You gave it Mom's voice!"

"Can you think of a better one?" Dauntless shot back.

"Enter PB One," Theresa instructed, running to the door. The hatch divided and the robot flew in. It was much bigger than Theresa had imagined. It resembled a hummingbird more than a bee. "What do I do now?" she asked Dauntless, but it was her bee that responded.

"I am your personal remote connection to Prodigy," it answered.

"Bring me a cola, PB One," Theresa instructed. She was walking about the command center with PB One flying six inches above her right shoulder.

"I am sorry. I do not possess that capability," PB One apologized from the top of the intercom console where it had landed to await Theresa's next move.

"Come on T, it's not a toy," Dauntless scolded. "Please, can we finish so we can go to breakfast?"

"Chill," Theresa said, touching PB One and hoping it would trigger a response. It didn't. It felt like cold metal.

"PB One, can you make yourself warm to my touch?"

"Theresa!" Dauntless began, but was interrupted by PB One.

"Touch me and let me know when you're satisfied," PB One instructed, lifting itself from the console and hovering over Theresa.

"Thank you very much." Theresa placed her finger on the robot and, when she was satisfied, she whispered, "Perfect." The heat sensor shut down. "Can you change colors?" Theresa looked at her brother with her finger to her lips, instructing him to be quiet. At the same moment, her phone buzzed and PB One spoke.

"I installed an app to your phone. You may use the functions any time you wish." Theresa had her phone in hand before PB One finished and was already changing its color to pink. She moved the color intensity dial with her finger until she was satisfied with the shade. *This is going to be fun.*

Dauntless had moved to the navigational table. "Prodigy, display Clementine maps." The hologram images of Earth's moon taken by NASA satellites came to life on the invisible vertical screen in the center of the table. "T, come have a look." He used his index finger to push through the maps on the screen until he found the one he wanted.

Theresa leaned on the table. "What have you got, Dauntie?" she said, giggling.

"Cute." He pointed to the sectional map of the Orientale Basin located on Earth's moon. "Our original plan was to deploy eight hundred miles above that location, but last night I got the premonition that we might be picked up by the Passnit probe."

"I thought that antique was offline."

"The Russians said it was, but now I'm not so sure." He flipped through more map pages on the hologram screen and stopped at the one viewing the Aronnis Plains of the dark side of Earth's moon. "I think we should deploy there. Less chance of being seen by probing satellites."

"Your glow star thingamabob hasn't been wrong yet. Will our altitude be the same?" Theresa asked.

"Eight hundred miles should be close enough. We only need a few hours, providing we don't have any problems deploying the robot cubes," Dauntless answered.

"And we don't burn to a crisp during the quantum particle entanglement speed," Theresa said, her eyes fixed on Dauntless.

"Have I ever given you bad information?"

"No," Theresa answered. "But I'm not as fearless as you. I'm a little afraid." She paused, looked away from her brother, and said softly, "A lot, actually."

Dauntless put his arm around her and squeezed her shoulder. "You don't have to go, T."

"I didn't work for six years just to chicken out at the last minute." She patted her brother's hand. "Let's go to breakfast."

"Just help me for a few more minutes," Dauntless insisted. "You start the check off procedures. Plan on departing in forty-eight hours. I'll enter the new coordinates. Then Prodigy will take over."

With those tasks finished, the siblings looked at each other in silence. Then in one voice they said, "When are we going to tell Mom and Dad?"

Theresa headed for the exit. "Let's play it by ear," she suggested.

Dauntless followed. He thought of his friend, Stone, trying to connect with him through telepathy, but received no answer. They exited on ground level and were greeted by a warm breeze sweeping over their faces. The trees were alive with new colors. It had been a long hard winter and it was refreshing to walk about with no coats or jackets. He walked to the embankment overlooking the dairy farm and stood in silence. In a moment of thought he recalled that day he broke his leg skiing down this hill. Trying to cheer him up while he was recuperating, his dad suggested he name it Broken Bone Hill.

The sun was low in the east and its rays were glittering off the metal barn rooftops. "I'm going to miss this place," Theresa said, reaching for Dauntless's left hand. She touched his new thumb. "Does it hurt?" she asked.

Dauntless shook his head. "No, it's fine," he said, giving her hand a slight squeeze. "We'll come back often," he assured her.

They turned and began to walk to the golf cart. Dauntless stopped to look at Building Thirteen. He knew the comments and jokes his employees were making concerning the weird shape of the building. It was best for them to think of it as ugly instead of trying to figure out what it really was. The structure was oddly shaped and the multiple levels seemed to be stacked haphazardly, at incongruous angles. The construction was done in modular stages and transported to Broken Bone Hill for assembly. Each contractor had a specific job to complete and was never allowed full access. It would be difficult for any of them to fully understand what they were constructing. Background checks for surveillance and security employees were extensive. Top secret clearance was essential.

Once in space, this ugly duckling would deploy into the *Arowon One* space station. Theresa called it a giant transformer in refence to the *Transformer* movies they had watched together as kids.

"You want to walk? It's a beautiful morning," Theresa said, stretching her arms high above her head.

"Sure. Don't have many more under these skies. Ow. What was that for?" Dauntless said, rubbing his arm where Theresa had punched him.

"I just want to enjoy the morning. Get my mind off everything for a while," Theresa said. She grabbed her brother's arm and pulled him close.

They walked in silence, each deeply in a trance with their own thoughts. Dauntless's mind drifted to the night he received the glow star and how amazed he was to hear Stone's voice while holding it in the palm of his hand. Over time, he discovered that the slightest thought of his friend could lead to a connection of minds, no matter how far apart they were in the universe. Stone could accept or reject the impulse. *Stone*" he thought.

Chapter Three
One hundred and fifty thousand miles out from the planet
Marsha, Andromeda Galaxy

What's going on, my friend? Stone answered.

Dauntless motioned to his sister. "You go on ahead," he said.

"It's him?" she asked.

Dauntless nodded.

"I'll meet you at home," Theresa said, leaving Dauntless standing on the side of the road.

You got a few minutes? Dauntless thought to Stone.

I always have time for you, old friend. Stone engaged with his friend while fidgeting with the viewfinder and trying to get a close-up of the planet Marsha. His craft was flying steadily and he estimated it would be one hour until he would begin his descent. He was on his second run from the mining planet, Ursa, where he had been born and raised. His craft was loaded with his parents' belongings to move them to their new home. His mom had been waiting a long time to return to her birthplace and he loved seeing the glow in her eyes in anticipation. His dad had been governor of Ursa and served the alliance honorably for twenty-two years. He had just been elected high potentate of Marsha. The ceremony was thirty moon rotations away and his mom wanted to be settled into their new home so she could entertain their friends and dignitaries.

Ahhh, just for fun, if I wanted to meet you tomorrow where would you be? Dauntless stammered, walking off the roadway into a rocky field. He chose a large flat boulder overlooking the dairy, climbed up, and sat down. *Actually, I want to… Ahhh.* He was hesitant to tell his friend what he was planning. You just don't pop across the universe uninvited without disrupting the status quo.

You OK, my friend? I'm getting strange vibes, Stone said. He dialed two hundred on the viewfinder's magnification and the surface of Marsha exploded on the screen.

Dauntless broke off a small twig from a bush that was growing awkwardly in the middle of the boulder and began chewing on it. There were a dozen cows grazing in the grasslands below, and he smiled as he remembered Stone had named them pouch bags so many years ago. Stone was Billbet back then, a lost and afraid ten year old, who had accidently travelled across galaxies and landed on Earth. They were together only a few days but in that short time they'd formed an unbreakable bond. *Is there a place we can meet tomorrow without my arrival causing any chaos? I have a few surprises for you.*

Stone leaned back into the pilot seat, crossed his arms, and stared at the ceiling lights. Thinking it was one of those what if games they often played when trying to figure out a complicated assignment in cadet class. He answered. *Well, I'll be on Marsha in sector LL17. But your arrival there would sure spook the locals. Might even get you arrested. So, if we were to meet, I would choose Galvena. One of the moons of planet XZL444. Nobody ever goes there.*

Dauntless spat the twig out. Took a deep breath. *OK, it's*

Galvena then. Give me the solar coordinates I need and I'll wait for you there. Dauntless slid off the rock and began pacing around the boulder.

In his spacecraft, Stone leaned forward and quickly stood up. This is not how the game is played, and his friend was not one to joke. *Where are you now?* he asked.

Earth. I know it must sound crazy but I can be there tomorrow with the accurate coordinates. Would you be breaking any rules if you gave them to me? Dauntless asked while walking back to the roadway leading to the farmhouse.

Stone checked his instrument panel and was satisfied that his craft was set and locked on course. He walked over to the window and gazed out over the stars. It had only been a few hours since he had awakened from the induced coma and it felt good to walk about his craft. *The trip is across four galaxies. So, it's impossible. Now tell me what's really going on.* They were both silent for a while. Stone thought first, *Dauntless, did you break off connection?*

Dauntless tried to explain. *I developed a way to get there. I want to try it tomorrow. If it works, I see great things ahead for us. If it doesn't, well, who knows what will happen.* Dauntless regretted not blocking the last part as soon as he thought of it. He could see the farmhouse now. He stopped walking, not wanting to arrive home while he was still communicating with Stone.

How is it that it will take me two moon rotations to get to Galvena, and that's if I leave right now, and you will be crossing four galaxies and be there before me? Stone asked.

Dauntless could feel his friend's confusion. He needed to choose his words more carefully. *Think about what we are doing right now. The slightest thought of you brings our minds together. Instantly, with no hesitation. I developed a transport that can achieve the same results.*

What we're doing now is a form of telepathy. There's a far stretch from transferring thoughts to moving objects across the universe. Anyway, we're only communicating because of the energy sphere my dad gave you, Stone answered.

Sphere, glow star, whatever you want to call it, has guided me step by step in the development of the transport system. I trust its capabilities with my life. Not wanting to expose his thoughts about Theresa to his friend, Dauntless broke off their mind intermingling.

Stone remembered that Dauntless had given him countless designs to new technology and had never been wrong. In fact, the information he provided had advanced his career. The alliance rewarded him well based on his friend's work. But to travel across the universe in less than one moon rotation was too much for his imagination to conjure. Not wanting his friend to think he didn't trust him, he decided to appease him.

A slight thought impulse from Stone reconnected the mind blend. *Galvena is a free zone, so no one will care if you hover off the surface, provided your ship doesn't have any exposed weaponry. Let me know when you arrive. It will only take two rotations for me to arrive.*

Dauntless realized immediately that his friend had doubts, but it was understandable. After all, what he had proposed was pretty far-fetched even to an advanced civilization like the Marshians. *No weapons, my friend. My craft has the number one written on all sides. It stands out like a beacon. When you're in range, I will guide you aboard.*

You really think I need guidance? Stone answered,

moving back over to his control station to get a reading on his entry time to Marsha.

I know you don't. I was just trying to save time. The craft is three hundred ninety meters long and has forty launch and capture bays. I'll deploy a tracking beam when I have a visual of you. Give me four long red flashes off your port so I can position you accurately.

I'm getting very concerned, my friend, Stone began, but Dauntless cut him short.

Trust me! You're worrying needlessly. I'll be a few Earth hours above the surface of our moon to fully deploy and then I'll let you know when I'm on the way.

Stone broke off again. Dauntless had gotten his imagination excited, and it would be fantastic to be with his friend once again. Thanks to thought transference they had experienced a brotherly relationship over the years. He longed to return to Earth to visit his friend but all his requests were denied. Earth was a restricted planet, even with his dad's influence, the alliance stood firm in their decision. He asked the navigational computer for the coordinates for Galena's dark side.

Stone reconnected. *Did you get them?* he asked

Got them. Thanks. Anything I should be concerned about with that location?

No. You got enough to worry about traversing four galaxies. May the Great One be with you. I'm in descent to Marsha, keep in touch. Stone broke off contact.

Stone could not stop thinking of the conversation with his friend. Twice during the descent, he had to shake himself free from dwelling on how outrageous the idea was. The alliance constantly updated information on habitable planets and there was no indication that Earth had the technology to send any of its population to other planets. If Dauntless broke the many barriers needed to accomplish this exploit, at the speed he was suggesting, it would far surpass the alliance capabilities. It might also put his friend in danger. The alliance did not like to upset the status quo. He needed to talk to his dad as soon as possible. His attention was drawn to the hologram viewer where his mom had just appeared.

"You made good time," Kimina said when her son's craft entered her radar identification beam. Having verified the craft's proper protocol, an all-clear advisory was transmitted, allowing its unimpeded approach. "Were you able to fit everything?"

"I squeezed everything in. It wasn't easy. I could hardly get off the launch pad," Stone said in a playful voice. "What's for dinner? I'm starving."

"Carson steaks are ready."

"My mouth is watering. That's why I love coming home," Stone answered.

"Let's relax over dinner before unloading. It's so exciting. Aren't you excited?" His mom sounded thrilled to be back on her birth planet.

"I am! I am! But most of all I love seeing you happy. Is Dad home?"

"Oh. You haven't heard? He was called to go to Miranda. Something to do with one of the mines."

"What about the celebration?" Stone asked.

"It's been postponed. To be truthful, I'm pleased, because I have more time to prepare."

"OK, Mom. I'll see you soon."

"May the Great One be with you," Kimina answered.

Chapter Four

There wasn't much for Stone to do during the landing except stand by in case the autopilot malfunctioned. He was presently above Marsha's frozen northern pole which covered thirty per cent of the planet. He remembered how astonished he'd been when he'd first caught sight of the massive mountains with their peaks jutting eight miles into the atmosphere. It was a far cry from the cave complex that was his home on the mining plant, Ursa.

Nunda, one of three moons that orbited Marsha, was off his port side. Its radiant side was flooding light to the ground below. Both Marsha and Nunda rotated on their own axes, creating day and night for the only inhabitable continent named after the planet. The glowing side of Nunda was super-heated by its galaxy star and, when facing Marsha, gave the planet life.

Stone gently moved the joystick controlling the on-board telescope and pointed it towards the planet's equator. He magnified the view of the one-mile hole in the ocean's floor created by a meteorite impact millions of years ago. A trillion gallons of water cascaded over the circumference of the abyss every second. The falling water dropped a mile below the surface of the sea. It flowed into two massive underground rivers. One flowed west and came to an abrupt dead end thirty miles from its origin. The tremendous water pressure found a weak section of the ocean floor and erupted into a three-mile trench forcing the river to geyser one thousand feet into the air all along the trench. Thousands of creatures flew constantly above the geyser, catching fish in mid-air that had been too weak to overcome the fall's current.

The second underground river flowed three thousand miles north. It also ended abruptly, erupting through the surface of the planet and propelling trillions of gallons of seawater eight miles into the air. Over millions of years, the water had frozen and formed the mountain. As the water continued to be forced up the center of the mountain, it had poured over its east side and froze. Every seven to ten minutes the weight of the frozen ice would collapse, sending an avalanche nine miles into the super-heated spring below. The ice melted within minutes and created the largest known wetland in the universe. The heated water stretched six thousand miles north to south and ten thousand miles west. It became home to ninety per cent of living creatures on the planet.

Stone forced himself away from these fantastic views to concentrate on his craft's entry into its final landing approach. The craft gently glided to a halt atop a landing platform on the seventh level of his parents' new home. With the craft secured, he exited onto the platform and stood at the railing overlooking Lake Vinta with its beautiful glowing waters tinted with a tad of green from the minerals flowing from the mountains to the north. On its eastern shoreline stood the city of Zen, the capital of the alliance. The videos of the planet that his dad had shown him over the years did not do this fantastic place justice. As he admired the view of the lake, the swish of the elevator door brought him back to reality.

Kimina walked in and stood next to her son. She was four inches shorter than his six-foot-six frame but her slim body made her appear taller. Her long blonde hair tied in a ponytail swung below her lower back. Her light, greenish brown skin showed no signs of aging. She had grown up around the lake, and swimming in it and drinking its water caused her green tone to be more intense than her son's. Lake people were always greener.

"Isn't it beautiful?" she asked. They touched foreheads and remained in the embrace.

Stone whispered, "I love you, Mom." He stood back to look at her. "I see you have your work clothes on." She was wearing a bright red pantsuit fringed with white lace. On her wrists were several jeweled bracelets. Atop her head sat a diamond crown. But it was the ten-carat sapphire around her neck that caught his attention.

"My job is to delegate," she said, waving her hand in the air. "Your father bought that boat." She pointed to a large cabin cruiser tied to the dock below.

"When is he ever going to have time to enjoy that?" Stone turned and leaned on the railing with his back towards the lake.

"Oh, I don't know. He's planning on having more time after he's installed as the high potentate. But I don't believe it. Can you even understand why they would call the elected potentate to a mining planet? It makes no sense." Kimina shook her head, clearly agitated. "Look at me. Getting all in a dither over something I have no control over. Let's go eat. I want you to tell me all about your new assignment."

"Close the bays," Stone instructed the computer. The steel doors silently concealed the huge hangar. "Do you remember

Kevin?" he asked, walking into a large foyer.

"Of course. He's that boy you met on Earth while you were stranded." She paused and looked towards her son. "Is that the right word? Oh, well, you know what I mean."

Kimina entered the hallway leading to a large empty silver room. She passed her hand over the wall on the right and a portion of it disappeared into the floor, revealing a massive stash of jewelry. Hair pins, necklaces, bracelets, rings, crowns, eye diamonds, ankle bracelets, the rows went on and on. She began removing the jewelry she was wearing, carefully placing it on the proper perch.

"Why did you bother putting them on? Seems a waste of time," Stone said.

"There's probing holograph satellites all over. They would just love to get a glimpse of the potentate's wife looking scruffy."

They entered the dining room. A thirty-foot table made of one gigantic piece of tacona stone excavated from the nearby mountains occupied the center of the room. The top had been smoothed and polished to a glowing yellow using saffron dust. Two place settings were meticulously arranged at the far end. But the enormous table looked uninvitingly naked.

"Sit at the head," Kimina instructed. She turned and began walking towards the kitchen.

"Mom. Why don't you hire someone to help you? This place is too much work for one person."

Kimina came back carrying a tray and placed it in front of her son. "I can manage. Besides, I don't want anyone snooping around, listening to every word your father and I are saying. Anyway, Rodas will arrive in a few rotations. Once he programs the androids, I'll be fine. Now tell me all about your assignment."

"First, can I tell you about Kevin?" Stone pressed.

"I don't like thinking about that. Do you know that your father was almost dismissed over that incident? The only reason they allowed him to continue as governor was because he paid for the rescue."

"I didn't know that," Stone said, gazing into his mom's stunning green eyes.

"Of course not. Your father would never say anything to you. And giving that boy an energy sphere, that took a lot of explaining. I offered the Great One everything to get you home." They both sat silent. "Eat before it gets cold," Kimina demanded.

While they ate, Stone told his mom all about his friend and how the energy sphere had kept them communicating over the years. He explained cadet school, and that Kevin was given the name Dauntless for his fearlessness in life threatening situations. He told her about his recent conversation and explained his concerns.

Stone placed his utensils gently on the edge of his plate. "I'm leaving for Galvena as soon as he contacts me. I have twelve rotations before I report to RR114 so I have plenty of time." He gave his mom a hard look. "Am I paranoid for being so concerned?"

There was quite a long silence. When Kimina finally replied, she completely ignored the question. "Rescue and retrieval. I pleaded with the Great One that you would go in that direction and not a military unit. Your father is going to be ecstatically happy. I can't say that I'm pleased about you going aboard the decrepit 114. But then the entire rescue fleet is old and slow."

Stone began bringing the dishes to the kitchen. "I agree, but the rest of the fleet doesn't have the prestigious history that the 114 enjoys. Besides, it's temporary. I've been promised the command of 332 as soon as Tesel retires."

"Good luck with that. The old geezer will never leave. I believe he's more in love with the military unit assigned to him then he is with rescue." Kimina started to help her son clear the table but he placed a hand on her shoulder so she would stay seated.

"You better tell your father," Kimina said, loudly enough for Stone to hear.

"Tell him what!" he yelled from the kitchen.

"About your friend. It could be an embarrassment for him."

"In what way, Mom?"

"Really, Stone. Think. Your friend traverses galaxies, what, seven times faster than the alliance is capable of and you don't envision powerful heads turning. And he's from a restricted planet."

Stone perceived the concern in his mom's tone. "But the restrictions were non-military."

Kimina stood at the entrance to the kitchen to get her son's attention. "It makes no difference why the limitations were imposed. The alliance command will not react favorably. Everything you have told me could place your friend in danger. He's from a restricted planet, he somehow has overcome speed boundaries, and from what you have described, he has unlocked the secrets to the use of the sphere. That third tidbit will send the alliance members into panic mode. They have been conducting experiments with billions of our population, for over a thousand years. No one has been able to overcome

42

the purity of soul needed to master the sphere's full potential. There was one breakthrough that provided a glimpse into its potential but that ended with great disappointment. If your friend is capable of having the very essence of his existence focused on benefiting the population of the universe and not allowing one iota of self-gratification then he has accomplished what seemed impossible. So, the only question will be, is he a friend or foe to the alliance?"

Stone hunched over in silence and collected his thoughts. "I know in my heart he is a sincere friend," he said without hesitation.

Kimina placed her forehead onto her son's. "The alliance will want to interrogate him extensively. They won't listen to you. They will demand to know who else he has shared these revelations with. They need to make an accurate threat assessment. There is something else you're not taking into consideration."

Stone thought about telling his mom about the many times Dauntless had given him the designs to new technology but decided this was not the time to expose the guilt he was feeling from profiting from someone else's discoveries. His friend had made him promise never to reveal the true source of the information. But the truth would provide the proof of his friend's intentions to the alliance.

"What's that, Mom?"

"You would be jeopardizing your career before it even begins."

"Mother, you're overreacting!"

"Oh, really? There are a half million surveillance satellites throughout the galaxies. One will definitely monitor your visit with your friend. Even if you miraculously avoid detection, how are you going to explain to the alliance your location that will be recorded on the tracking device that is mandatory on all spacecrafts?"

Stone knew his mother was right. This was getting too complicated. He would instruct his friend not to come.

Chapter Five

Theresa leaned over and gave her mom a long hug and kissed her on the cheek. "Good morning," she said.

"What about me? I'm the one who made breakfast," Frank said, holding the spatula high.

Theresa gave her dad a kiss on the cheek.

"I want you to know you and your brother are making us very nervous," Frank said.

"What is that thing hovering over your shoulder?" Marian asked. She was used to the kids bringing all sorts of new gadgets to the table so she wasn't particularly concerned. Marian reached for her daughter's arm and gently pulled her close. "Dad said you are getting close to the end of your project. Is he right?"

Theresa instantly noticed the worried frown on her mom's face. She sat down at the table and held her mother's hands between hers. PB One settled onto her left shoulder. She was torn between love for her parents and the importance of what she and her brother were about to do. She desperately wanted a way out of telling them that they would be leaving in a few days. She removed her right hand and touched the robot.

"Good morning, Mrs and Mr Kensey. I am so pleased to finally be in your presence. I am even more joyful that I find you both in superb health." PB One hovered above Frank and then gently flew to Marian. "To answer your question, Mrs Kensey, I am Theresa's personal connection to the main computer located aboard the *Arowon One* space station." PB One floated around Marian a few times. "I find that you and your daughter have the most perfectly matched DNA that I have had the pleasure to observe, making it difficult to know to whose command I should respond."

"Oh, my God, it sounds just like you, Marian," Frank said.

Marian smiled. "I don't sound anything like that. Let it talk. I like what it's saying." She squeezed her daughter's hand. "I always knew we were identical," she whispered.

Theresa drew in a deep silent breath. PB One had taken her mother's mind off of the project.

"May I ask it a question?" Marian asked Theresa.

"Sure, Mom. You can ask PB One anything."

"PB One, is the spacecraft ready for flight?"

Frank quickly answered. "Marian, let the kids decide when to tell us."

"I'm just worried," Marian said.

Theresa continued to squeeze her mother's hands, then lowered her head onto them and remained silent.

Prodigy, detecting a heightened distress emotion in the DNA of Theresa and because of his continued mastery of human emotions, instructed PB One to fly over and land on Marian's shoulder. PB One whispered into her ear and within a minute a smile filled her face and the worried frown disappeared.

Frank placed a dish loaded with scrambled eggs and bacon in front of Theresa. No one spoke.

Dauntless shattered the silence. "Awful quiet in here," he said as he cheerfully entered the kitchen. "What's going on?"

"Dad told Mom that we are almost finished with the project," Theresa said, releasing her mother's hand.

Dauntless bent and hugged his mom.

"I already know, Kevin," she said, unwilling to free him from their embrace. She knew all about cadet school along with the new name but refused to abandon his birth name. When she closed her eyes and thought of Kevin, her son filled her mind; when she thought of Dauntless, no visions came to her. Kevin is Kevin and that's all there is to it, she thought.

Dauntless placed three small silver boxes on the table and a leather briefcase on the floor next to his chair. He sat next to his sister. "Morning, Dad," he said, motioning for him to take the chair next to his. He looked at his mom. A joyful smile flooded his face. "We finished. We're set to leave in a few days."

Marian reached out and held her husband's hand. Quiet filled the room. Marian's eyes were fixed on her son's. "Why?" was all she could manage without a flood of emotions escaping.

Dauntless and Theresa held their mom's and dad's hands. Dauntless was the only one who spoke. "I have so much to share, but most importantly, I have so much I need to learn," he said softly.

"Why can't you work with NASA and let trained astronauts go? You and Theresa could work with them from here." Frank's eyes were pleading for his son to agree.

Dauntless slowly shook his head. "We as a planet are not ready. Most of the world is still in conquest mode. I can't share this yet."

Marian spoke so softly that Dauntless had to lean towards her to understand. "Are you one hundred per cent sure that they are not looking for a conquest?" she asked.

Dauntless knew she was referring to the alliance.

"They would have already done so," Dauntless said in a comforting tone. "I need to learn what I can and discuss with their leaders how they maintained peace. My dream is to bring their successful ideas back home."

His mom's eyes filled with tears. "I don't want to lose either of you."

"We will talk to you both every day," Dauntless assured her.

He handed the three of them a small silver box. "Inside is a sliver of the glow star. Slide the cover," he instructed while flipping his thumb to reveal the rest of the star. Light exploded into the room. "Gaze into each other's eyes and when you experience a feeling of comfort, turn and look at me." Slowly, each turned to him. "When you want to talk to one another, merely think of whom you want to communicate with and you will be in contact, just like a video chat on your phone."

Dauntless handed his dad the briefcase filled with hundreds of inventions and instructions on how to implement them. "Release four or five of these schematics a year to our technical department. They will know what to do. There's a folder marked 'government'. Give that to any officials who might come snooping around after we leave. The contents will satisfy them for a while."

"Exactly where are you going?" his mom asked.

"First, we are going to coordinates located on the dark side of our moon. We will deploy there and then meet Stone. You know, Billbet."

"I know who Stone is," Marian interrupted. "What do you mean deploy?" she continued.

Theresa flung her arms into the air sending PB One flying to the top of a kitchen cabinet. "I've got a great idea," she said. Her cheerfulness infected everyone. "After breakfast, we will take you to *Arowon One* space station. We can show you everything, and then you can watch a video which will show our deployment step by step. When you see what we have done, you will be less fearful."

"Now that's an excellent idea," Dauntless agreed.

Chapter Six

Building Thirteen (*Arowon One* Space Station) Broken Bone
Hill: Kensey International, Schuylerville, New York

"How tight are these straps supposed to be? I don't feel any
oxygen flowing." Theresa could feel herself losing control.
"How am I going to see with this stupid fishbowl I'm wearing?
I've never heard of anything so stupid as riding vibrating
stings. Not to mention the idiotic idea that there is such a thing
as particle entanglement."

Dauntless unlatched his harness and went over to Theresa.
He removed her helmet and bent close. "Take a deep breath.
Now let it out slowly." He gently kissed her forehead. She
grabbed his hand and pulled him close. "It's normal to be
apprehensive," he said.

"I'm such a coward, Kevin," Theresa said, her lower lip
quivering.

Dauntless raised her chin and removed the tear from her
eye. "No, you're not, T. You are the most courageous person I
know. You have accomplished more than most people have
done in a lifetime." He gave her another kiss on the forehead.
"Just close your eyes and in a few seconds, we'll be looking
down at Earth. Oh, by the way, I'm Dauntless," he whispered.
She smiled and punched him in the arm.

**

BOOM----BOOM

The first sonic boom was the breaking of the sound barrier. It rattled a few windows. The second shock wave came when *Arowon One* passed through light speed; that shock wave broke every window on every building in the complex that faced west.

Prodigy log entry:

May 7, 2020 at 02.11 hours 13 seconds Earth time. Located at Kensey International, Schuylerville, New York the Arowon One Space Station departs Earth. Sound barrier broken at 02.12 hours 45 seconds.

May 7, 2020 at 02.13 hours 19 seconds Arowon One space station surpasses light speed at an undetermined multiplier.

May 7, 2020 at 2.19 hours 01 seconds Arowon One space station arrives at predetermined flight station. Coordinates provided by NASA: AZ0012005 – Balta Euclidean Plain (Klein bottle intersection real projection plane Victor 09902516738-R77.)

**

Arowon One Space Station: on location, dark side of Earth's moon.

Dauntless looked towards his sister. "You can open your eyes now," he chuckled.

"Holy cow. Is that the moon?" Her gaze was fixed on the planet filling the navigation window.

"You OK, T?"

"Ya! Can I take this dang helmet off?"

"Just hold for a minute," Dauntless instructed. "Prodigy, any damage to the ship?"

"All systems operational. No damage detected. Your oxygen and simulated gravity are one hundred per cent," Prodigy replied.

"Thank you. Display all archived video of our journey captured from the exterior cameras," Dauntless instructed while removing his flight gear. He glanced towards T who was already free from her restraints.

Theresa was moving from window to window. "I thought we would be able to have a view of Earth," she said.

"Let's fully deploy and then we'll sneak around the moon and you'll have your view."

Prodigy broke the silence. "There is no video of our journey, Captain."

"That's impossible," Dauntless countered. "Figure it out when you can, but first initiate full deployment of *Arowon One* using predetermined protocol."

"Yes, Captain. I will display each robot cube as they become operational."

"Thank you."

"By the way, Captain, during our journey we collected thirty thousand hours of energy."

"Now we know the collectors and storage equipment are functional. It seems like a lot for such a short trip. What was the time of journey?"

"Approximately seven minutes and three seconds," Prodigy fired back.

"Whew!" Dauntless exhaled. "Why approximately?"

"There is some confusion with the deciphering code

52

between the vibrating strings aligning the particle entanglement justification. I am working on the accurate solution, Captain."

"Very well." Dauntless had been totally immersed in his activities that he had completely forgotten about his sister. He looked but could not locate her on the bridge or in navigation. "Prodigy. Do you have Theresa's location?"

"Yes, Captain. She is in engineering with PB One."

No sooner than having said that, the intercom blared, "Dauntless, we have a slight problem. Meet me in engineering."

"On my way T. Prodigy, do you show any malfunctions?"

"None, Captain."

Dauntless entered the engineering compartment and found Theresa hunched over a huge bank of switches, levers and buttons. She was flicking a switch on and off in rapid succession. He reached over and held her hand to stop her.

"I decided to check the entire ship to make sure there were no problems and then I ran into this." Theresa pointed to the monitor screen displaying the exterior views of the starboard side of the ship.

Dauntless flopped into the chair next to his sister. He manipulated the joystick, zooming in on a giant robot cube that had failed to fully deploy. He displayed the ship's maps onto an invisible screen to his left.

"It's my relaxation room, the French Riviera. It's airtight but the left magnet is not attached. I really need that area." His sister was pointing to the map. "See it there."

Dauntless magnified the camera view and inspected the area in detail.

"Stop!" Theresa shouted. "Zoom in on this," she said,

pointing to the censor located at the far end of the robot cube. "It's detached and joined to the locking control censor. That's why Prodigy wasn't notified."

"I see it. Look further down. That glide shaft is bent. Do you see it?" Dauntless said, leaning back into the soft chair cushion.

"Oh ya. How the heck are we going to fix that?" Theresa's face was inches away from the monitor as she studied the image. "No! No!"

"I'm afraid so. There is no other way," Dauntless said, touching his sister's shoulder.

**

Arowon One Space Station: Space walk

Dauntless could clearly see his objective. It appeared to be a mile away. In reality, it was less than five hundred feet. He yanked on his harness for the tenth time. The air hatch door was opened but his mind refused to step out into the void of space.

"Is everything OK?" Theresa asked. She was watching her brother on a series of digital pan, tilt and zoom cameras that were strategically positioned both in and outside the craft.

"Aeeee, I'm kind of looking for the nerve to step out," he admitted.

"That's OK. Take—" Before she had finished her sentence, her brother stepped from the open airlock hatch.

Dauntless slowly depressed the button located on the side of the small computer that was attached to his protective suit. He began to move towards his objective. He was attached to two nylon tethering ropes. One line would be used to transport any tools he needed. The other was his lifeline. Both lines would be attached to the craft once he reached the location. The other ends were secured to the inside of the airlock. As he slowly moved forward, he realized how quiet it was, to the point of being eerie. He and his sister had spent many hours in the simulator practicing walking in space, but nothing had prepared him for the fear that was swelling inside his mind. He was shaken back to the present by his sister's frantic voice coming through his headset.

"For God's sake, please answer me! What the heck is wrong out there?" Theresa screamed.

"I'm OK! I was overwhelmed, that's all."

"Well, don't do that again. You scared the life out of me."

"Sorry! I'm OK now." He was at the damage site. He secured both lines to the hull with digital magnets and began to inspect the damage.

Ten minutes passed in silence. Dauntless spoke first. "The guide rod is distorted so badly that it cannot be straightened."

"That's not good news. Any ideas?" his sister asked.

"Two options. We can leave it as is and not use this cube, or we can cut out the damaged section and replace it."

Theresa took in a deep breath. "What do you mean, we?" she asked, fearful of the answer.

"You know, T, this is not a high priority cube for our mission. So, you have to ask yourself how badly do you want this cube operational. If you have your heart set on getting this cube up and going, I'm going to need you out here with me."

"Dang!" Theresa responded followed by a long silence.

"T, I need an answer. Plus, I want to get back inside."

"OK! OK! Let's fix it."

"Fine! I'm coming back in to get the tools and materials

we'll need. Get the sled ready and bring it to the airlock."

**

All the tools and materials were loaded onto the hover sled and attached to the tether line. Both Dauntless and Theresa were suited up and prepared to step into space. While getting ready, Dauntless had explained to his sister what needed to be done. They had to weld a titanium rod to a mega jack, then place it between the hull and the cube. There was enormous pressure on the damaged rod and this action would alleviate the possibility of the cube moving forward once it was cut out. The unknown factor was how the cube would react once the damaged rod was replaced and the titanium rod and jack securing the cube's forward movement was removed. If the cube violently moved forward, it could be devastating for both astronauts. Dauntless was calculating that he would be able to release pressure on the jack slowly enough to prevent any mishaps.

Dauntless stepped into space first. He turned and looked towards his sister. "It's time, T."

Theresa held tightly to the tether and eased her way into space. She instantly flipped and began to spin around the lifeline. She released her grip on the rope and, using both hands, grabbed onto the robot sled in front of her. Once she stabilized her movement, she was astonished at what she saw. She had never seen so many stars. The clarity of their brightness was amazing. The sensation of weightlessness pleased her. "I kind of like it out here," she admitted.

"Good to hear," her brother responded. "Let's get started. I'll do all the bull work. You just need to place the other end of the jack against the robot cube. Once I engage the jack, come back and get behind me."

"OK, Kevin," she said, her voice wavering with nerves. "Sorry."

"It's OK T. I'm anxious also. It's a heck of a lot different than the simulator."

"Really, I'm OK."

The two space travelers became entirely focused on their work. It wasn't until they had been in space for three hours that Theresa looked at the oxygen gauge. "We only have thirty minutes of oxygen left." Panic edged her voice.

Dauntless remained silent, focusing on the final layer of weld needed to repair the broken rod.

"Did you hear me?" Theresa raised her voice.

Dauntless pulled his welding torch away from the rod, and instantly the intense glow of the welding arc vanished. "Finished," he said, turning to his sister. "Move further down the lifeline. Bring the hover sled with you. I'm going to release the jack."

Theresa obeyed. "Be careful. Go very slowly."

Dauntless began to release the tension from the jack. As he did, he noticed that the pressure on the new rod was moving the robot cube towards the engagement keeper at the same speed. What he failed to see was the jack twisting. As the pressure on the jack decreased, it twisted off the edge of the spacecraft and sent it violently into space. The robot cube rapidly advanced forward towards the keeper, the corner of the cube severing the lifeline. Both astronauts were secured to the line. Theresa was further up the line closer to the airlock and was hanging onto both the lifeline and the secondary line. This prevented her from being jettisoned into space. Dauntless was not so fortunate.

"Dauntless! Dauntless! Kevinnn! Answer me!" she shouted.

Nothing but silence. She glanced at the oxygen. Twenty-two minutes remained. She realized at that moment that her brother had suited up first and that his oxygen level would be lower. To what extent, she could not predict. It was imperative to get to him. Was he alive or dead? The uncertainty sickened her. The urgency of saving her brother overtook her entire being.

"Prodigy, send a robot stretcher to airlock seven immediately."

"Number twenty-nine is the closest. It will be there in three minutes." Prodigy answered.

Theresa released herself from the lifeline while still firmly grasping the secondary line. She attached herself to the hover sled. Looking further down the lifeline, she could see that her brother was entangled, preventing him from being thrown into deep space. Thank God, she thought. After starting the sled, she released it from the secondary line. To her amazement, it did not go flying into space but simply floated in place, rocking back and forth. She removed all the tools from the sled and tied them to the secondary line. Now that the sled was empty, she manipulated the controls and began to slowly move towards her brother. Once close enough to the lifeline, she grabbed it and positioned the sled to move towards her brother.

She slowly rolled her brother over. Checking the digital readout on his wrist computer, she breathed a sigh of relief. He was alive but not responsive. The frightening reality was that she needed to get him to the airlock in six minutes. She latched him to the sled and began to cut through the entangled line.

That's when he began the uncontrolled shaking.

"Oh, my God!" Theresa reached for her brother and held on tightly. His shaking continued. "Got to get him inside," she said, talking to herself.

She cut a large section of the lifeline and tied her brother to the sled. Oddly, it helped reduce the shaking. She turned the sled and pointed it towards the airlock. In her eagerness to get to safety, she jammed the throttle forward, sending it on a high-speed collision course with the airlock hatch. Within seconds, the sled collided with the door frame of the airlock and sent them crashing inside to the far wall. The sled was still revved up and began twisting. Theresa let go of the thrusters and the sled went dead. She cut herself free and slammed the airlock door button. Once the door closed and she was sure that the room's air supply was replenished, she cut her brother free and removed his suit. She put him back on the sled and turned it on. Slowly, she manipulated the controls and lifted her brother high enough to roll him onto the stretcher. She was becoming light-headed and was having difficulty breathing. She fell to her knees, her head spinning, and realized she was about to pass out. It was then that she realized she had not removed her space suit. Her oxygen was depleted. She unlatched the helmet and sucked in the fresh air.

**

Dauntless lay lifeless on the stretcher. His shaking had subsided and all his vital signs were OK but Theresa was still unable to revive him.

"Theresa, may I suggest something?" PB One asked.

"Please!"

"I believe if you crack open a smelling salt cartridge and put it under his nose, that will do the trick," PB One offered.

Theresa did what PB One suggested and her brother shook his head. "What happened?" he demanded.

"I love you, PB One," Theresa said, jumping up and down.

The robot stretcher transported Dauntless to recovery room four, Theresa holding firmly to the side rails. Her brother had fallen asleep. She kissed his cheek, then left the room so he could rest.

**

Theresa returned to the recovery room and found her brother awake.

"Will you please tell me what happened," Dauntless demanded again.

After Theresa answered all of his questions, Dauntless took a deep breath. "Man, am I tired."

Theresa covered him with a blanket and kissed his forehead. "Get some sleep. I'll wake you in a few hours."

"I can't. We are already behind schedule." Dauntless sat up and looked at his sister. "What about you? How are you doing?" He swung his legs across the side of the stretcher. "I have to go back out and bring in all the tools."

"Shuuu! Everything is done," Theresa assured him.

"You went back out!" her brother said, astounded. He sat up quickly, only to become extremely dizzy.

Theresa gently pushed him back down. "I like being out there. Gives me clarity." She commanded the robot stretcher to take her brother to his quarters.

Chapter Seven

Arowon One space station: dark side of Earth's moon

"Prodigy. Locate Theresa."

"Theresa is in the dining hall."

Dauntless made his way to his sister and found her preparing table settings for both of them.

"Well, look who decided to rise and shine." Theresa hugged her brother and whispered in his ear, "Hope you're feeling better."

Dauntless gently kissed her forehead. "Thanks for saving me. You're amazing."

Theresa's face lit up. She love-punched him in the arm. "I talked to Mom and Dad. They want you to be in touch soon."

"Did you tell them what happened?" Dauntless said flopping into a chair.

"No way! That would just multiply their worries."

"Good. Did they have any news?"

Theresa continued to set the table. "Oh ya! Government officials flooded onto the property at sunrise. Dad gave them the papers you provided but that did not satisfy them. They had a court order giving them the authority to inspect the property. They found the location of the launch and started installing cameras, censors and recorders all over the property. Please touch base with Mom, she is worried sick."

"I'll do it now while you fix breakfast."

Theresa stood tall and fixed her eyes on her brother. "Are you really going to trust my cooking?"

"After yesterday, I trust you can do anything. Besides, your cooking has to be one hundred per cent better than mine. I'd rather you screw it up and not me."

"Oh, Dauntie, I love the way you express your confidence."

"After breakfast, I have a surprise for you," Dauntless said, teasing his sister.

"What! Tell me now," she pleaded.

"Nope."

Theresa stood close to her brother. Pressing herself against the chair, she said, "I would be carful eating the eggs."

"I'll take my chances." He stood and gave his sister a pat on the head. "Be right back. I want to talk to Mom and Dad in private."

"Remember, no secrets," Theresa demanded.

Chapter Eight

Arowon One space station: Earth view excitement

Dauntless was holding onto his sister's arm, guiding her. "This is ridiculous. Where are you taking me, and why the blindfold?"

"Hush! Be patient." He brought her to the observation deck and positioned her in front of one of the large windows. "Are you ready?" he asked.

"Yes! Hurry up!"

Dauntless uncovered her eyes. She was shaking with excitement.

She stood quietly. Tears filled her eyes. "It's so beautiful. I love you, Dauntless. Look." She pointed. "Is that a storm over Africa?"

Dauntless said nothing. He was enthralled watching his sister's reaction. She had both hands pressed against the window and her face was almost touching the glass. The deep blue from Earth glowed in her eyes. She was so beautiful, he thought, and PB One was accurate in saying she was a perfect match to his mom. At that moment, he realized how much of life his sister had sacrificed to help him with this endeavor. She had never had a male companion, no camaraderie with girlfriends, no real friends, ever. He scolded himself for being so selfish. He continued to bask in his sister's delight. Her entire face glowed and then he understood that this is where she wanted to be. The endless hours of exhausting work, the disappointments, one after another, and then the cherished feeling that can only come with success.

The constant chatter of his sister broke Dauntless from his daze. "I'm sorry, T, what did you say?"

"Have you ever seen anything so beautiful? Can we zoom in on the farmhouse?" She was giggling with excitement. "I love the way the clouds just seem to float about like a giant blanket. Did you ever imagine there was that much ice at the South Pole?"

Dauntless remained silent, enjoying his sister and her special moment. All that she ever wanted was to view Earth from space. She was so disappointed when he had changed the location to the dark side of the moon. Dauntless thought, *I could die right now but embracing this moment would make it all worth the effort.*

"Oh my God! That's Australia." She grabbed her brother's arm. "Do you see it?"

"It's beautiful, T."

"Wow, that cloud looks like a huge dolphin. Look at those amazing colors drifting over North America. Now that's something you don't see every day." She was moving quickly from window to window. "Do you see the smoke over there in California? Oh, my God, that has to be from wildfires. Do you see it?"

"Yes," Dauntless answered softly, not wanting to interrupt his sister's wonderment.

"You know, we should stay here till night falls and watch the city lights sparkle. Can we? Pleaaaase?"

Dauntless knew that they might be detected if they were to remain in this location. But he did not have the heart to refuse. Anyway, what could anyone do if they were detected? Nothing, he rationalized.

"Sure, we'll stay as long as you want."

"You're the best brother ever."

"I'm your only brother."

She punched him in the arm, never taking her eyes from Earth.

Chapter Nine

Arowon one departs for Galvena Moon, Andromeda Galaxy

Theresa was fidgeting in the co-pilot's seat. "I feel naked without my suit on."

"Prodigy said we didn't need to wear them. His information hasn't been wrong yet." Dauntless finished instructing the computer to proceed to the coordinates provided by Stone and to orbit eight hundred miles above Galvena. Particle entanglement would begin in thirty minutes.

"Oh, did you forget about the French Riviera?" Theresa gave her brother a hard look.

"Point taken." Dauntless said, purposely looking away from his sister, remembering that the computer had indicated that the French Riviera robot cube was fully deployed.

"Do you think he's going to like me or will he treat me like a dumb girl?" Theresa stopped twiddling with her safety harness, satisfied that it wasn't too tight. "I'm a bit nervous. I'm not sure how to thank him for saving Mom," she said to her brother. "Is that nitrogen gauge supposed to be reading minus forty per cent?" She tapped the gauge several times. She spoke at rapid fire speed.

"Relax, T. The gauge is accurate. I'm purging the fuel line. Stone doesn't know you are aboard. I want to surprise him, so stay out of sight until I call for PB One. That will be your signal to join us. OK?"

"I think it's stupid, but OK. What do I say? Should I hug him?" Theresa had flipped on the cameras overlooking Earth for one last look.

"Good lord, you act like you never met anyone before. Prodigy, do one last check of the ship's integrity."

"Yes, Captain."

"Anyway, T, Stone's not like that. Plus, I don't believe there is anyone in the universe that would not like you. I'll bet he has never actually met anyone who saved someone's life. As for me, you're the first one that I know."

"Ship is secured, Captain," Prodigy reported.

"By the way, Prodigy, were you able to retrieve the video I requested?" Dauntless was checking the exterior cameras and this reminded him of the discrepancy.

"No, Captain, I am creating a new program that might help explain the lack of video and also retrieve it. I am also creating a new pixel restoration program. The video of your spacewalk was archived perfectly, making me bewildered as to what went wrong on our journey. I am in the process of reorganizing the external camera programs to reflect the density of black matter and how our rate of speed affected the digital imagery."

"Very well." Dauntless was amazed at how rapid Prodigy was at gathering information. The computer's ability to multitask and learn and improve on its own aptitude had already exceeded the projections of its designers. Prodigy would reach singularity far ahead of schedule.

"I really didn't save your life," Theresa said softly.

"If I had been alone, do you think I'd be sitting here? You told me there were only six minutes of oxygen left. If getting me back into the airlock isn't saving my life then I have no idea what your definition would be." Dauntless felt a little annoyed that his sister was dismissing her achievement. "You could have frozen and done nothing. Countless people would not have had the courage to disconnect themselves from the lifeline. I watched the videos over and over and I would choose you to be with me in any situation. God, T, you took charge and put your life in danger. For me!" He tapped his chest several times. "You are my hero, now and always."

Theresa was looking straight ahead while her brother was talking. She turned towards him with tears in her eyes. "I'll always have your back. I promise."

They sat in silence.

"Are you ready, T?"

"What, to shoot across four galaxies? Oh ya!"

**

Arowon One Space Station: May 7, 2020 at 21.10 hours, 14 seconds, Earth time

Prodigy log:

May 7, 2020 at 21.10 hours 14seconds Earth time. Arowon One Space Station departed. AZ0012005 – Balta Euclidean Plain (Klein bottle intersection real projection plane Victor 09902516738-R77

Sound Barrier broken at 21.10 hours 45 seconds.

May 7, 2020 at 21.12 hours 19 seconds Arowon One Space Station surpasses light speed at an undetermined multiplier.

May 7, 2020 at 22.19 hours 04 seconds Arowon One Space Station takes orbit position eight hundred miles above Galvena Moon, Andromeda Galaxy

"God, that's the ugliest planet I ever saw," Theresa exclaimed. "But we are alive and well."

"Thanks for thinking of me," Dauntless chuckled. "Couldn't be better."

"T, you and PB One walk the ship while I check things with Prodigy. You are right calling this place ugly. Looks more like an asteroid than a moon."

"Sure, Boss," Theresa said, giving her brother a salute. "Let's go, PB One." The pink robot flew over her right shoulder as she exited the bridge.

"Prodigy, report on ship's integrity."

"Yes, Captain." Prodigy displayed the ship's maps onto the screen. "All robot cubes' indicators display a positive air lock, indicating no leaks. Oxygen and gravity one hundred per cent. All censors reporting no structural damage. All engineering capabilities one hundred per cent. I have a negative report on external cameras. They are operating and recording but I am still unable to view video of either voyage. Interesting information is that the electrical storage units report a seven-year accumulation. Is there any other information you would like me to access?"

"Not at this time. Can you explain the electrical power storage rate?"

"Yes, Captain. I have not yet been able to accurately determine our speed during our particle entanglement but the tremendous friction created from our forward movement indicates that it must have been enormous. The energy created

69

from the friction and gathered from black energy of space has generated power at an extraordinary rate."

"Are you willing to estimate our speed?"

"It would be in the range of one hundred million light years a second."

"You've got to be kidding!" Dauntless placed both hands on the consul as if just hearing the speed might make him light-headed.

"I'm sorry, Captain, I have not learned the art of kidding."

"That's OK, Prodigy, you will. Thank you."

Dauntless sat quietly and composed his thoughts. He watched his sister move about the ship tripping motion sensors, her image popping up on different monitors. He appreciated the detailed inspection she was conducting.

Who am I kidding? he thought to himself. *I'm just stalling from contacting Stone.*

He leaned back and closed his eyes. He began to re-experience his first encounter with Stone.

He remembered Molsen barking and wagging his tail so hard when he saw Billbet that his rear-end lifted off the ground. *God, I miss that dog*, he thought. Molsen had just wanted to be petted but it had terrified Billbet, who had been crouched underneath his window, bleeding, tired and cold. He must have thought Molsen was going to tear him apart! When Dauntless had tried to talk to Billbet, they could not understand each other. Billbet had given him a small clip-on device and motioned for him to put it on his ear. It took a while to realize that he wanted him to look into his eyes. Once they had locked eyes, they were able to communicate. That's the moment that he understood Billbet was from another world.

"OK, enough procrastination," he whispered.

Stone, can you talk? Dauntless asked repeatedly. He was about to give up when his friend answered.

Where have you been? I expected a contact from you sooner. I've thought it through, and I don't believe it would be prudent for you to move ahead with your plans, Stone answered.

Dauntless remained silent.

Dauntless are you there?

I'm already at the agreed upon location, Dauntless told his friend.

Stone pushed himself away from the desk he was sitting at. *Why would you do that? I was under the impression you wanted me to check with my dad.*

I know, but I am not going to let the possibility of detection interfere with my mission, Dauntless countered.

Stone sat down and tried to collect his thoughts. He remained calm and attempted to mask his annoyance. Over the years, his friend had mastered telepathy and the energy sphere allowed him to identify Stone's temperament. *What mission?*

Dauntless hesitated before answering his friend. Separating and compartmentalizing thoughts before transmission through telepathy was no easy task. Over the years, Dauntless had inadvertently exposed feelings that he would have otherwise hidden from his friend. He relaxed and took a deep breath. *I need to explain to you face-to-face. I understand the risks, and I understand you will be jeopardizing everything you have worked so hard to accomplish. I know I have no right to interfere with you achieving your goals, but the glow star has guided me to this endeavor. If, after I explain the mission and you do not wish to be at my side, I will relinquish everything over to the alliance.*

One thing the academy had taught Stone was to quickly process information and make a decision based on the facts, discounting any emotion. It was a fact that his craft was equipped with a tracking device, but the alliance had no reason to trace his movements. After all, there must be millions of such craft and the alliance only used this capability in unusual circumstances. Anyway, he was on holiday before reporting to his duty station and could go wherever he pleased. *Give me two rotations and I'll be there. Is your ship equipped with monitoring devices?* Stone said.

Yes, I have multiple sensors onboard. So far, I have not received any pings. Dauntless was moving about the bridge as he thought. *Two rotations, that's about six Earth days. Thank you, my friend. I am eager to see you.*

I'm also excited but still extremely concerned. Make a note of this protocol. XTFGTR453. I'll be transmitting that code so you can identify my craft. Stone was communicating but in a deeper mindset, he was planning his departure and explanation for his mother. Embarrassing his father was also a nagging concern. He decided he would deal with that when, and if, the situation demanded.

Chapter Ten

Orbiting surveillance modular SM77: Galaxy NGC3432

Surveillance Officer Jelani was a graduate of the most recent space cadet class. His parents had tremendous aspirations for their talented son and had pressed him hard to attend the prestigious Rullna Academy. Graduating in the top ten of his class would guarantee their son a command of the rescue department on the coveted new space station. There was no denying he was one of the hardest working students. He had studied continuously and had never hesitated to seek assistance, but it became more and more difficult for him to achieve the fortitude needed to be a senior officer. His extraordinary talent was limited to electronics and even his father's influence could not bridge the gap. So, after graduating, he had been stationed on orbiting surveillance modular SM77 where he gazed daily at hundreds of monitors, waiting for the sound of an alarm to be transmitted from any one of sixty thousand satellites blanketing detection coverage for his assigned section of the galaxy. Officer Jelani took his responsibilities seriously and only a rotation ago he had discovered, tracked and altered the path of a meteorite that was on a collision course with one of the alliance's space telescopes.

"Lieutenant, come take a look," Officer Jelani said, motioning to his commanding officer.

Lieutenant Kenji liked his new surveillance officer and was proud of his initiative adapting to his work duties in such a short period of time. Most of the new cadets assigned to him hated working on the small modular and would purposely screw up in an attempt to be discharged. This only assured their removal from any space program for life. Jelani was from a different breed. He loved to tweak the equipment to its limits. He was constantly requesting permission to interchange, interconnect or recalibrate devices as he tried to see further into the galaxy. His most recent request was to modify the speed sensors to satellite SS118972. He hoped that with this modification he would be able to identify smaller objects at further distances. Once he verified it was successful and relevant, he would write a protocol for all the satellites.

"What have you got for me, rookie?" Even though Kenji was satisfied with his fledgling, it was not his nature to give anyone a commendation.

Jelani speed typed on his computer requesting the exact time that he had witnessed the anomaly. It took only a moment for the computer to display the recording. "What am I looking for?" Kenji said, annoyed. "All I see is black matter."

"I'll replay it in slow motion," Jelani offered. The irregularity had moved from left to right across his monitor in a fraction of a second. Due to its speed, the cameras only captured a few hundred digital impressions. "Right there, Lieutenant," Jelani said, freezing the recording and pointing to what appeared to be a straight line across the screen.

"Have you gone space crazy, rookie? I see nothing. Before you go any further, you sure better explain what it is you think you see," Kenji barked.

Jelani leaned back and turned towards his superior. "I'll start the recording over. Keep a close eye on this side of the monitor." He placed a tiny mark on the monitor with a wax pen. "I'll run the recording at its slowest speed. What you will see is a movement in the black matter that I can't identify. I calculated the speed at one hundred million light years a second."

Jelani started the recording.

"I still see nothing. Enough with this foolishness." Kenji turned and began to leave Jelani's workstation.

"Sir! Can't you see the wave-like movement?" Jelani pressed.

"Of course, I do, rookie. It's an electrical glitch. Stop bothering me with such nonsense." Kenji walked away, wondering if his prized new surveillance officer was becoming disgruntled like so many of his predecessors.

Jelani shrunk into his cushioned chair. Normally, he would be able to back track this wave to its origin by tracing the movement across thousands of satellites, but the modification was programed only to satellite SS118972. The wave was not captured on any other surveillance recordings. He felt defeated. Why couldn't the lieutenant understand that this sure wasn't a malfunction of the monitor. He pushed away from his workstation, disgusted with himself for not being able to persuade Kenji that what was captured on the recording should be investigated more thoroughly. His failure ruined his opportunity to recommend his new protocol to the alliance. He watched the video of the anomaly and changed the speed, starting with slow motion and then systematically increasing the speed. When the video was running at top speed, he was convinced that he was witnessing an invisible object moving through black matter at an unprecedented speed. He stood away from his workstation. Looking towards the surveillance officer to his right, he asked, "Barkan, will you cover me for a while?"

"Sure. You OK? You look a little peaked."

Jelani walked out of the surveillance room without answering. He sat at one of the two tables in the small break room trying to compose his thoughts. Had he just witnessed travel through another dimension? Aerospace engineering and engineering mechanics had always been a source of wonderment to him. The investigation and experimentation of vibrating strings and particle entanglement were an urgent priority for the space program, but the funds allocated to it dwindled at each conference with the absence of any meaningful advancements. The cost of development was staggering, especially with absolutely nothing positive to report and useless pieces of experimental equipment left to rot in warehouses across the galaxies.

Jelani walked the short distance to the pantry and passed his identification badge across the scanner. The clear door disappeared. He grabbed a snack and liquid pack and took the four small steps back to the table. He popped the liquid pack and raised it to his lips. He froze for a few seconds before lowering the container. His mind was reeling with questions. What if no one ever explored the possibility of travel through another dimension? What if vibrating strings and particle entanglement could only be attained while in a different dimension? How did the object in the wave enter the dimension? Had any of the gifted engineers in the program even thought of such a possibility? If so, would he be able to access the data? He started back to his workstation determined to continue his investigation in his time off. He would have to disregard alliance regulations and risk being removed from the space program, but the opportunity to discover a new dimension far outweighed his personal goals.

Chapter Eleven

Arowon One Space Station: orbiting Galvena moon,
Andromeda galaxy

Beep-beep---beep-beep--- beep-beep

"Captain, contact off our port. Trajectory intersection between our coordinates in twenty-five minutes." Prodigy's message broadcasted throughout the spacecraft.

Theresa, startled from a sound sleep, jumped up and ran towards the bridge, with PB One following over her right shoulder. "PB One, identify contact."

The beeping warning changed to a screeching siren.

"Sensors detect that we have been pinged. Unable to identify contact. I am projecting video from the port telescope," Prodigy reported.

"Very good, Prodigy." Theresa took control of the optical scope and manipulated it in real time. "PB One, locate Dauntless and bring him here." The robot bee flew off.

"Theresa," Prodigy interrupted. "I have no communication with the captain's sleeping quarters. My records indicate that there has been no power in that sector for six hours."

"Why didn't you report that earlier?" Theresa demanded, as she slowly manipulated the telescope throttle and brought the contact into perfect focus.

"With all due respect, Theresa, that information is

proprietary."

"What in the world does that mean? What information can you offer on the contact? Dauntless is not on the bridge so I'm in command. Restore power to the captain's sector immediately." Theresa fired commands to the uncooperative computer. "What are you up to, Dauntless?" she whispered.

"I will answer your questions and requests in the order you presented them. Proprietary in this context indicates the captain's desire that the information you requested be denied," Prodigy stated.

Theresa continued to peer through the scope to view the contact. "I know what proprietary means. What I don't know is why."

"I have no indication as to the captain's intentions. I have information regarding the contact. It is a small spacecraft. I estimate four-passenger capability. It is powered by chemical rocket thrusters which give it a max speed of about eighty thousand miles per hour. I detect thirty-three separate electronic signatures emanating from the craft. The strongest originate from two ion thrusters. When active and in unison with the main propulsion rocket, the craft can easily obtain hyper speeds."

Theresa's eyes were fixed on the images the telescope was transmitting. The craft would intersect with their orbit in less than twenty minutes.

Prodigy continued. "Theresa, I am unable to give you a command, therefore, I am not authorized to grant your request to restore power."

Fear swelled up in Theresa and her anxiety was making her dizzy. She placed both hands onto the console, closed her eyes, and with every ounce of her willpower she commanded her body to calm down. After taking deep breaths and exhaling slowly, she felt a calmness overtake her. When she opened her eyes and looked at the monitor displaying the telescope imagery, she jolted out of her chair. The unidentified craft filled the screen. It was too late to take action. She flopped back into her seat. Somewhere in the back of her mind, she could hear a voice. Once again, she demanded her mind to take control.

"Theresa, Dauntless is in his sleeping quarters and all access has been denied," PB One said, taking position over Theresa's right shoulder.

Theresa felt defeated. She fixed her eyes on the craft that appeared to be minutes out from their location. That's when she realized that earlier she had requested two hundred times magnification. She recalibrated to zero and the craft faded into the darkness. "Prodigy, how much time before we intersect with the unidentified craft?"

"Assuming its speed remains the same, nineteen minutes and thirty-three seconds."

Theresa sat up in her chair. I still have time, she thought, releasing a breath of relief. She began to prioritize her situation. First and foremost, she had to protect them from any threat that might originate from the unidentified contact.

"Prodigy, I am issuing a protocol command Dauntless Versus Theresa PC777. Initiate without prejudice."

"Command protocol initiated. Theresa number 401-00-112 in command, time, date and circumstances duly noted in log number CRD111," Prodigy replied.

"Very well. Plot an evasive course using vibrating strings and particle entanglement. Hold orbit until further instructed. Also scan contact for military armament. While you're at it, hack into whatever electronics are aboard that thing, but don't compromise until I give authorization." *That should give me more time to locate my brother*, she thought. This was the first time she had felt in charge since the incident began.

Prodigy instantly responded. "Evasive course one light year beyond contact. Awaiting your command. The craft has no exterior military capabilities. It is possible that weapons may be hidden but the design of the craft makes it more likely a commuter vehicle rather than an armed one. I will report periodically regarding compromising the crafts electronics."

Theresa sighed in relief. "Prodigy, restore power to all sectors." Her tone indicated a direct order rather than a request.

Prodigy calmly stated, "I am unable to comply with your demand."

"Prodigy, I want you to assume that Dauntless is unable to fulfill his duties and, for the safety of the ship and all aboard, I command you to restore power to all sectors," Theresa shot back, annoyed.

"I am unable to comply."

"Very well! Prodigy, activate laser to PB One. Full power." *We will see who's boss*, Theresa thought.

"Laser operational on your command."

Theresa inhaled deeply. Her next command could have serious consequences to the integrity of the ship. She exhaled slowly. I'll give it another try, she said to herself. She left the console and moved to stand in front of one of Prodigy's main frames. "Prodigy, execute course change when contact is minus five minutes from intersection. Once again, I order you to override all other previous commands and restore power to all sectors."

Lights flashed across the computer's main frame that she

was standing in front of. "Course change protocol minus five minutes from intersection. Your request to restore power to all sectors is denied."

"OK! I have no other choice," Theresa said. "PB One, go to Dauntless's living quarters. Burn through any hatches that deny you access. Video everything and display onto monitor three-seven-seven."

"As you wish, Theresa." PB One flew off the bridge.

**

Much to Theresa's surprise, she was relieved to hear Prodigy announce, "Power restored to all sectors."

Theresa immediately requested video from the cameras located in her brother's sector. Even though there were no cameras in his living quarters, she was eager to see what was happening in and around the area. "PB One, have you located Dauntless?" She jumped, startled by her brother's voice.

"I'm right here, Sis." Dauntless had just entered the bridge, PB One hovering above.

"Where have you been?" Theresa demanded.

"Just observing," he shot back, a grin engulfing his face.

"You are a real jerk. We have a severe problem. We've been detected and the dang thing is about to intersect our location." Theresa grabbed her brother's arm and dragged him to the telescope monitor.

"It's only Stone," he answered calmly.

Theresa's face burned with rage. "You knew all along," she yelled and punched him has hard as she could in the stomach.

Dauntless doubled over. "Oww! Holy cow, will you calm

down?"

"How could you? Why would you?" Theresa shouted.

"Prodigy, I'm resuming command. Disregard evasive action protocol." Dauntless had turned away from his sister and was unprepared for the punch to his kidney. He held the console tightly to prevent from falling. He shook off the blow and turned towards Theresa. "Calm down."

Prodigy interrupted. "Dauntless is in command, time date and circumstance duly noted in log number CRD111."

Theresa turned to exit the bridge. "Get lost," she said.

Dauntless ran towards his sister. "Sorry! I wanted to witness how you would react during a crisis." He held her shoulder and slowly turned her around and held her tight.

"You're an idiot!" she sobbed. "I thought something had happened to you. I imagined all kinds of crazy stuff."

"I'm sorry! I really am, but you did fantastically even with all the junk I threw at you. You've got to feel good about that." He slung an arm around her shoulder.

Prodigy interrupted the moment. "Contact intersection minus five minutes.

"I got to get ready. Make yourself scarce like we planned."

Theresa pushed away from her brother.

"No more punching," he said, smiling.

She glared at him, turned and left the bridge.

Chapter Twelve
Old and new friends

Stone reached over and pressed the alarm warning him that his vessel had been detected. He was troubled that Dauntless had not established communications. The spaceship filling his telescope was huge. But Stone was even more astonished by seeing *Arowon One* displayed across the entire craft. *What are you up to, Dauntless?*

Stone's attention was diverted by a screeching siren. He silenced the alarm and sat frozen. Was his friend actually trying to hack into the ship's computers? No, this must be a mistake, he thought. He rechecked the protocol signal he had given his friend. XTFGTR453 – transmitting perfectly. He had already displayed four long red flashes off his port side. Had Dauntless gotten it wrong? He powered down to minimum speed. He slowly increased magnification to the telescope. With the increased magnification he could see through the massive windows of what had to be the bridge. "Holy Great One," he said softly. He intensified magnification, tweaking the focus until he had a clear image. He choked away a sob and fixed his gaze upon his friend. The boy that had saved him so many years ago was now a handsome man, staring out the window of his spacecraft and looking confident and commanding.

Dauntless could now see his friend's craft without the use of the telescope. *Ahoy there, my friend. Switch to zero-seven-seven-nine-nine frequency so we can talk in real time,* he instructed.

Stone dialed the appropriate frequency. *I am astonished you're here.* He clicked on the intercom and walked over to the small window to get a better view of the massive craft that lay off to his stern. "Quite a feat, my friend. That's one impressive ship."

"It's hard to express how excited I am that we are together once again," Dauntless said, fighting against his emotions.

"You named her Arowon One. What are you up to, my friend?"

"All in good time. Let's get you aboard and then we can relax and I'll fill you in. Follow the tracker beam and enter cargo bay twelve. You can secure your craft to pad one. I'll airlock and meet you there. It's great to talk to you without using telepathy."

Dauntless instructed Prodigy to transmit throughout the ship so his sister could hear. He grabbed two colas and headed to bay twelve.

Stone moved back to his control panel and took his ship off of autopilot. "Roger that. I have a visual of bay twelve. By the way, are you compromising my computers?"

Dauntless's face filled with delight knowing what surprises he had planned for his old friend. "No! But that is a long story. One of many!" He was now at Bay twelve and sitting at the control's console viewing the cameras that were strategically placed inside the bay. He had instructed Prodigy to take command of positioning Stone's craft into the hangar.

Once the visiting craft was secured and Prodigy had airlocked the bay, he gave Stone the all clear to exit. Stone opened the door to his ship and stood in the doorway.

A deafening alarm filled the bay. Prodigy's warning filled the air. "Unidentified DNA detected. Bay twelve locked down."

Dauntless was startled at the intensity of Prodigy's declaration, and it took a moment for him to recover. Stone stepped back into his craft.

"Prodigy, override DNA alarm. Log new sample and identify as Stone," Dauntless commanded. The alarm silenced.

Dauntless opened the inner bay door and walked over to meet his friend. They grabbed each other with a tight bear hug. Both started talking at the same time, then burst into laughter. Stone held his friend's shoulders and looked into his eyes and smiled broadly. "By the Great One, you look fantastic."

They stood in silence, each gazing at the other for a moment. "We've come a long way from the farmhouse where we first met," Dauntless said, breaking the stillness. He put his arm around his friend's shoulder and guided him out of bay twelve. As they exited the bay, he picked up the two colas he had placed on the console and handed one to Stone. He held his high to begin the toast. "To us and our new adventures."

Stone clicked his cola, then took a long swallow. He smiled in ecstasy. "I can't believe you remembered how much I loved this stuff. It seems like it was only moments ago we were in your bedroom and you talked me into trying this marvelous liquid. Remember, we were both blubbering idiots."

Dauntless pulled his friend close. "I got a couple of pallets for you, along with the recipe and ingredients in case you want to share with your friends."

Stone patted his comrade's back. "Now that's how one maintains lasting friendship." They clicked their colas again.

"PB One, it's time," Dauntless blurted.

Stone looked at his friend confused. "Who's PB One?"

Dauntless shrugged. "It's a surprise."

**

The door to the bridge was already opened. Stone stood frozen just outside the entrance. Dauntless was at his side, grinning and thoroughly enjoying his friend's amazement. "Is that... " Stone began to stammer.

"Yes! Yes! Yes!" Dauntless said unable to conceal his excitement. "Stone, this is my sister, Theresa."

Theresa stood silently in front of the massive windows, a binary star in full view behind her. The star had burst a million years ago, sending multicoloured fragments billions of miles into space and creating an elliptical firework display. Theresa had inadvertently positioned herself directly in the middle of the star's center, giving the appearance that she was totally engulfed in its awesome power. PB One, hovering above her right shoulder, added to the illusion.

Stone recovered from his astonishment. He approached Theresa and held out both his hands, palms up. "I am so pleased to see you again."

Theresa's heart was pounding. She was enthralled with this extremely handsome man extending his hands towards her. Without taking her eyes off of Stone, she asked her brother, "What did he say. I can't understand."

"Dang," Dauntless said softly. "Stone give her an ear node."

Stone removed a node from his bag and handed it to Theresa without ever taking his eyes off of her. He was totally lost in her beauty.

Theresa held the node in the palm of her hand, gazing at Stone in utter disbelief that she was finally meeting him. Her brother took the node and placed it on her earlobe. "Look into his eyes so your minds can blend," he instructed.

Theresa regained her composure. "Do I really want my mind blended with yours?" she said, smiling, and then gave him a slight punch in the arm.

Stone stepped back and gave Dauntless a bewildered look. "It's an action of endearment," Dauntless explained to his friend.

Theresa's face turned scarlet. "I'm so sorry. What was I thinking?" She grabbed Stone's arm and began to rub it gently. "I have been waiting a long time to meet you. My brother never stops talking about you. Billbet did this, Billbet did that. Oh, sorry, I mean Stone." Theresa realized she was squeezing Stone's arm tightly and let it go. "I'll stop talking now."

Dauntless stood to the side, taking in the magic happening between the two.

Stone, six inches taller, looked down into her eyes. The excitement of her touch was lingering. "Let me fix that." He adjusted the ear node. "There. How's that?"

The surprise of understanding his words did nothing to mask the unfamiliar pleasure of his touch. To her amazement, she felt embarrassed and spoke flippantly hoping he wouldn't notice. "Guess our minds are blended. Better be careful what you think."

Stone held Theresa's hand. "I am thinking about a young girl I stole a glimpse of so long ago. The image of her beauty burnt into my mind. Now here she is, standing in front of me, more beautiful than my imagination could ever conjure." Then he punched her in the arm. A bit too hard.

"Ow!" Theresa yelled.

"Sorry!" Stone said.

All three burst into laughter.

"OK. OK. Let's get serious. I have another surprise," Dauntless said to his friend, pulling him by his arm and positioning him in front of Prodigy.

"Prodigy, I am turning command of *Arowon One* over to Stone. As of this moment, he will be Captain Stone. I will assume second in command. Theresa holds succession of both positions."

"Protocol logged," Prodigy responded.

Theresa ran to Stone and threw her arms around him, engulfing him in a tight hug. "I'm so excited for you!"

Stone reluctantly broke from Theresa's embrace. He turned towards Dauntless. "What are you doing? This is crazy. What are you saying?" Stone looked slightly dazed, as if he were unable to comprehend what had just happened.

Dauntless put an arm around his friend's shoulder. "I am giving you *Arowon One*."

All Stone could think of to say was, "Why?"

Dauntless guided his friend to the windows in front of the flight chairs. "You have been complaining for the last eight years how old, how slow and how inadequate the rescue and retrieval fleets are, so, knowing your passion, I wanted you to be in command of the best ship anywhere in the known universes." He held up both his arms as if he was engulfing all the majestic stars filling the endless darkness. "Pick a planet, my friend. You can be there in a matter of minutes to render assistance. It will be challenging but fun choosing your crew, and once the alliance understands the capabilities of this ship, they will make the brightest and most talented people available for your consideration. Theresa and I designed and engineered every detail. We believe that the glow star guided us to develop the most advanced rescue craft ever to be built both now and far into the future. It is our gift to you. We pray you will accept it and allow us the honor of being your first crew."

Stone gazed out into space. A billion stars flickered in every direction. The binary star explosion filled the window on his right. The trapezium cluster containing Orion's four hottest and most massive stars glowed brightly in front of him. To his left, he could clearly see Barnard's Merope Nebula with its beautiful color array. He inhaled deeply. "You were always so generous." He turned and looked into Dauntless's eyes. "If it wasn't for you, I would never have graduated with honors. The dreams we talked about were only dreams for me. I never believed I would achieve any of them." He hugged his friend and whispered, "I was dreaming while you were doing." He stood apart and warned Dauntless and Theresa. "The alliance will never allow me to command this ship. They will take it by force if they have to and arrest both of you."

Dauntless placed both his hands on his friend's shoulders. "Come on, now! You must know I planned for just that. You let me worry about the federation and the alliance," he said with such confidence that Stone felt relieved for the first time since coming aboard.

Theresa gave Stone a soft punch. "Feel better, Captain?"

Stone shook hands with both of them to cement the agreement.

"I'll let you two rehash old times. Show him around," she told her brother. Theresa turned to exit the bridge. She said, loudly, "Give Captain Stone a bee." She turned swiftly. "Hey, Captain, meet me at the French Riviera in an hour. Ask your bee to show you the way."

Chapter Thirteen
French Riviera

"PB One, play 'Runaway' by Del Shannon," Theresa commanded, moving a lounge chair closer to the surf.

As I walk along, I wonder what went wrong with our love a love that was so strong. And as I still walk on, I think of the things we've done together while our hearts were young. I'm a walking in the rain, tears are fallin and I feel a pain wishing you were here by me to end this misery.

"Louder, PB One." She stood overlooking the Mediterranean Sea. "Bring the temperature to ninety-one degrees," she instructed. "Yes, this is perfect," she whispered. It was the first time she had entered this level since all the robot cubes had been deployed.

"PB One, bring in high tide. Oh, bring the sun to eleven a.m. position." She remembered how she had argued with her brother and tried to convince him that a swimming pool was just not enough. She reminded him that there would be twelve hundred personnel living aboard once *Arowon One* was fully staffed, and they would need a place to relax and calm down. It was the second time they had disagreed since beginning the project. The first disagreement was when he wanted to name the ship *Arowon One*. Then felt awful when he explained it was the Marshian word for 'rescue'. She had had a dream detailing every inch of the cube's design and was determined not to settle for anything less.

"PB One, bring in a cool breeze from the west. We need soft white clouds while you're at it. Make them small. No! No! I don't want them to hide the sun. Perfect."

She had hired a team of architects from Cannes, France to duplicate seven hundred feet of its French Riviera shoreline, including hotels, restaurants, theaters, sidewalk cafes, boardwalks, cabanas, and hillside apartments. Not one detail was overlooked. She even imported truckloads of sand from the beaches of Cannes and designed robots to rake the beaches when not in use. All that was easy compared to the mechanical engineering and computer programing needed to control environmental conditions on command.

Theresa was a god when in the French Riviera. Temperature, weather, sun, clouds, sounds, colors, all bowed to her will. Her mood would determine the experience she would enjoy on any given day at the beach. In order to make this dream a reality, she needed to add another level to *Arowon One* which would extend the full length of the ship and be on the top level. She recalled how nervous she'd been just before handing her brother the estimate costs. Her palms were sweating, her stomach ached and her head pounded. She was sitting at the farmhouse table fidgeting with the sizable stack of papers that comprised the bid. Her brother, sitting next to her, looked concerned. "You OK? You look sick."

She'd taken a deep breath and passed the bid to her brother. She'd vowed to herself that she would not argue but agree to whatever changes he wanted. She reached under her chair and handed him the rolled blueprints. "Let's look at these first," he said, unrolling the stack of prints and placing a bowl on each end to prevent them from snapping closed. "Ummm, adding an entire level. That's bold. Ahhh, not calling it level fifteen but French Riviera. Different but sounds much better."

Theresa took another deep breath and let it out slowly and silently. *So far so good*, she thought, but he hadn't seen the price.

Her brother reviewed each print in silence. Theresa attempted to read his body language but he was so dang cool she got nothing. He removed a bowl and allowed the prints to snap back into a roll. He flipped through the bid contracts quickly, not lingering on any particular page. He turned his chair to face his sister. "You know I love you and would do anything for you," he said, gazing into her deep brown eyes.

"Oh, OK! What does that mean? Is it a go?" she blurted, feeling as though she was about to beg for his approval. Her brother did not speak. "OK! I know six hundred fifty million dollars sounds high, but we're creating an oasis in the middle of nothingness. You said that we will most likely be in space for years on end, and this will give the crew a release from the boredom. Plus, the hospital patients will heal faster having this beautiful setting to take their minds off their injuries." Her hands were visibly shaking, and she could feel herself getting emotional.

Dauntless took both of her hands in his. "Calm down, Sis. Heck. You know you can have whatever you want."

"So, you just wanted to see me squirm?" She pulled both her hands away.

"Well, Sis, I do enjoy messing with you."

She got up and hugged him for a long time. And that was that. She'd started the project the next day.

Theresa lay on her lounge chair. She was wearing a pair of large pink sunglasses that matched her two-piece bikini. Her long black hair flowed over the back of the lounger. Her tan was smooth and uniform.

"PB One, play it again but louder." She loved this song. It brought back memories of when her Grandfather would drive around for hours trying to put her to sleep, this tune blasting over and over. She knew the words by heart.

Prodigy had finished programing high tide and the surf was now breaking just below Theresa's lounger. She dangled both feet and enjoyed the warm surf flooding back and forth. This was the first time she had felt totally relaxed since leaving the farmhouse. She began to envision Stone. She had not expected him to be so dang handsome, and what the heck was that strange feeling she had gotten when she met him on the bridge? Then she realized she was smiling.

**

Theresa jumped from her lounge, startled. "Woow! You scared the heck out of me." She was blushing now, standing in front of Stone.

Stone grabbed Theresa to prevent her from stumbling face first into the surf. "I am so sorry. I did call your name but this pleasant sound is very loud."

"PB One, stop the music," Theresa commanded, but made no attempt to back away from Stone. She felt her blush growing warmer but there was nothing she could do about it.

"Thanks for saving me," she said. She pointed to a cabana to her left. "Go put a swimsuit on. I'm sure you'll find one that fits. You do swim, don't you?"

Stone released her even though he did not want to. "I do. This is a beautiful place. Is this where you go on Earth?"

Theresa walked into the Mediterranean Sea until it covered her knees. She turned towards Stone. "I saw it in a movie once and always wanted to go there but never did. The truth is, I've never gone anywhere. This is the first time I've been away from home."

Stone smiled. "Well, you sure made your first trip a long one."

Theresa remained silent, not wanting to lose the softness of his eyes. Finally, she spoke, knowing that whatever she might say would destroy the moment. "That's for sure. Go get a suit on."

Dang, there's that feeling again, she thought. "Find a pink one," she yelled to Stone. She walked up and down the beach, never taking her eyes off the cabana.

When Stone came out of the cabana wearing a pink suit and walked toward her, Theresa took in a deep breath. *Oh, my God, what a beautiful man. He must work out constantly. He's even more muscular than Dauntless! And that tan. No, it's not a tan, it's more like a slight tinge of green but so seductive.*

Stone stood with both hands in the air. "Pink. I guess it's your favorite color."

"Yes! But it looks so much better with your complexion." *Dang! That feeling is back.*

Theresa held her hand out. "PB One, come." The bee landed on her hand. "Touch it," she offered to Stone.

"Feels so real," he said.

"You didn't bring PB Two?" Theresa raised her hand high and her bee flew off to hover above her shoulder.

"I told it to wait outside." Stone looked over his shoulder

towards the entrance. "Your brother showed me the video of your space rescue. It was a daring feat. I have to admit I was afraid for both of you. I didn't think you were going to make it."

Theresa blushed. "Anyone would have done the same thing."

Stone looked at her with a hard gaze. "Don't ever make light of your achievements. I don't know very many men who I would trust to release a lifeline to save me. But you're top of my list."

Theresa lowered her head. "Thanks," she said shyly. "Did my brother tell you I was with him during every cadet class?"

"Yes, he just told me a few minutes ago."

Theresa stood tall, sun lotion glistening on her bare belly, arms and legs. She took a step towards Stone. "I want a name," she said defiantly.

Stone was caught off guard. He was so infatuated with her appearance, he had not understood what she asked.

"Well?" she demanded, smiling at him as he gazed at her longingly.

Stone shook off his trance "Ahhh, huuu, what did you say?"

Theresa drew her shoulders back to show her full figure. "A name. I want you to give me a name. Is that so hard?" She was watching his eyes and it was apparent he was confused. It was evident he was not listening but trapped into looking and unsure whether to take his eyes off of her or answer the question.

It seemed like an eternity but he finally answered. "A name. Ahh, yes." He moved to her, removed her sunglasses and placed his forehead against hers.

95

"What are you doing?" she asked in a non-threatening tone, not wanting him to stop.

He slid both hands through her hair. "Shuuu!" he whispered. His warm breath flooded over her face, sending a delicious thrill through her entire body. "I'm feeling your mood," he said. Theresa closed her eyes. The feeling was back, but she melted into it. "Nula!" he said with confidence. "You are Nula."

"Who is Nula?" she asked. "It is a beautiful name."

Stone lifted his forehead. "Nula is the possessor of all beauty throughout the universes, dispensing it as she wishes."

Theresa's eyes flickered. "Goddess," she said softly.

"Ahh, yes," Stone answered.

"I love it. I thought you would give me a name for bravery or something macho. But I just love the sound of Nula."

Stone stood back and raised both hands high. "I proclaim that from this moment you will answer to the name of Nula, no other."

Nula, lost in the moment, kissed him on his lips. She felt something wonderful swell within her and nearly collapsed in his arms. Her head fell to one side, her heart pounded so loudly she wondered if he could hear it. She had only kissed one other man, Nicolas Signor, a twenty-five-year-old computer programmer who had worked at Kensey International. In the movies, the girl would melt into her lover's arms and they would be happy forever. She'd been sixteen with no social life and had longed for this fantasy. But the kiss with Nicolas had been empty and had left her unmoved. After, he would not leave her alone. She'd transferred him to the Duluth office.

The glorious moment with Stone ended, and they parted. She was so confused, she blurted something she regretted as soon as the words left her lips. "I do feel your mood."

He ignored the comment. "What was that for?"

"I wanted to thank you for saving my mom. Besides, I just wanted to."

A frown crossed his face. She placed a finger on his lips. "No! No! I've wanted to thank you for the longest time but my brother did not want to spoil the surprise by you knowing I was around."

"I remember your mother vividly. I cried when she got out of bed free from her injuries." Stone kissed Theresa on her forehead. "How is she?"

"She's perfect."

They waded into the Mediterranean Sea until they were waist deep. "PB One, play, 'I Drove All Night,' by Celine Dion. Play it softly." As they listened to the music, they held hands and splashed each other with their feet. "You like this song?" Nula asked.

"I have never heard such things before but, yes, I like it." Stone dove headfirst into the surf. Nula followed.

They frolicked for a while and then walked out and stretched out on lounge chairs. They remained silent, each lost in thought. Nula felt both euphoric and melancholy. She missed home and already longed to see her mom and dad, but she also felt excited about today. She never thought she would meet someone, least of all someone from another world. She wanted this day to last forever. Could it?

"Did you know what your brother was up to?" Stone asked, shattering her moment.

"Sure. We tell each other everything." She shrugged. "Well, almost everything."

Stone sat up. "Do you two have the slightest idea of what

you have accomplished? I've been told since the day I was old enough to talk that Earth was so far behind in technology and social acceptance, that it had no chance of being accepted into the alliance anytime in the foreseeable future. Yet here you are. You show up in a craft far superior to any in the alliance. You travel at speeds I can't even imagine. I knew the energy sphere was powerful. But I am also sure no one ever expected your brother to master its secrets." He shook his head and a worried expression filled his features.

Nula reached for his hand. "I trust Dauntless without question. He has never disappointed me. Sure, we disagree sometimes, but he always takes the time to explain why I should consider his point of view."

Stone smiled. "Oh! You do disagree."

"Well, really only once. When he wanted to name the ship. I didn't realize what the word meant," she admitted.

"Did he explain?"

"Sure. It means rescue."

"That's true but not the whole story," Stone said, pleased he could tell the tale. "Each letter represents a word. *AROWON* stands for *Asellia vobon ovento wizabon onitila nuonabona*. It's a Marshian folk tale about one who transcends civilization from darkness and suffering into the light of redemption. My father read me this tale many times as I was growing up. It is why I chose a rescue assignment over a military carrier, which would have been more lucrative."

Nula gently kissed his hand. "Then I guess my brother chose perfectly. Tell me about Marsha," Nula said, tilting her head to see the soft inviting color of his eyes.

Stone frowned. "My dad, Zada, and my mom, Kimina, were born and raised on Marsha, but I was born on Ursa." He turned his wrist computer to show Nula the videos of the vistas he had witnessed on his descent to his parents' house. He pointed to his new home and then displayed photos of his mom and dad. "I've only been to my parents' home so I can't speak much about anything else." He reached for her hand. A smile filled his face. "We'll explore Marsha together."

Nula did not speak. She squeezed his hand. "Kimina is so beautiful, just like you."

The doors to the French Riviera opened and PB Two flew in. Two messages came at the same time.

"Captain, we have been detected." PB Two was hovering in front of Stone's face.

"Hey, guys, we've been pinged," the voice over the intercom declared in a calm voice.

Chapter Fourteen
Orbiting Surveillance Modular SM77

Surveillance Officer Jelani stretched, then looked from side to side to see if anyone was watching. When he was satisfied that he was in the clear, he placed the tiny ball into the pocket of his bag. His shift was almost over and he barely had time to finish downloading information from seven more surveillance satellites. His palms were sweating and his neck kept twitching, a sure indicator that he was extremely nervous. Once his replacement arrived, he headed straight to his bedroom. As he passed the break room, his friend yelled, "Jelani, you up for a game of tonk?" He did not bother to answer. All he could think of was how far behind he was. He needed to review the information on the memory spheres as quickly as possible. Every moment he had it in his possession increased the risk of his scam being discovered.

He threw his sack onto his cot, walked over to his computer and placed the stolen memory sphere into the proper compartment. Instantly, a multitude of configurations appeared on the hologram screen. Each one represented a contact alert that one of the three surveillance workstations had recorded. Normally, the surveillance officers working one of the three workstations would receive a signal (in real time) indicating an object had entered their sector. This would prompt a detailed investigation. All information would be logged and video saved.

Jelani's hands were shaking so much it was difficult for him to enter his crypt code. His neck began to spasm violently. It forced him to lay down until the contractions subsided. He drifted off. Visions of him shackled, arrested, and shamed in front of his family filled his mind. He saw his friends and heard them whispering, *Traitor! Spy! Conspirator!* He woke with a jolt. Had he gone too far? he wondered.

He received the contact signal early in his shift. The alert was picked up at workstation one, but the program he had secretly installed at each position blocked anyone from receiving it. Instead, it was sent to a recording sphere that was hidden at his workstation. The program interceptor recorded many contacts, but most were useless, the typical space fragments that were of no concern to anyone. But this one was very different. The ping was definitely bouncing off a large metallic object. He quickly reviewed the log. There was no notification from the alliance of any spacecraft in that sector. He downloaded information from the seven nearest satellites in the chain and anticipated viewing the unknown contact along its path.

Jelani splashed cold water over his face and tried to clear his mind. He went back to work at his computer. The fear of being discovered weighed heavily on his mind, and he had to force himself to calm down. His attention was focused on the contact from Surveillance Satellite SS10000. Once he opened the panel, three cameras flashed a red signal which indicated a contact had passed within their parameter. He ran all three videos simultaneously. As SS10000 slowly drifted around Galvena, *Rescue One* came within camera range. Jelani jumped up and froze, dumbfounded.

He knew of no *Rescue One*. The ships of the alliance were *Rescue* and *Retrieval*. He wondered, could this be the newly commissioned space station? Then he was shaken to his core. *Rescue One* had vanished. He played the video over and over, at every speed. The results never changed; the ship had just disappeared. The fastest ships in the alliance could reach warp three but the surveillance equipment could easily track them.

Fear overtook Jelani. He was about to call his lieutenant but stopped cold. He struggled to make a decision. How would he explain to Kenji why he had the memory sphere? He paced the tiny room, wringing his hands. Then there was the program interceptor and the unauthorized download of his speed program onto all the satellites in the sector. What have I done, he thought?

**

In his private quarters, Lieutenant Kenji splashed cold water over his face. He put the stopper in the sink drain and ran the cold water. He put two ice packs into the sink, leaned on the basin, and watched as the sink filled. His shoulders collapsed as he thought about his conversation with Admiral Natan. He had regretted calling him as soon as he'd heard his voice.

He plunged a towel into the ice water and let it soak up the frigid liquid. *Stupid air conditioner. What good is a repair division if they can't even fix a simple condenser?* Satisfied the towel had sucked up as much cooling nectar as it could hold, he draped it over his head, moved to his favorite chair and fell into it, totally defeated. "Idiot Jelani!" he heard himself saying out loud. He leaned back into the soothing head restraints, not caring that he was soaking wet. "Arrest! They're going to arrest him," he said aloud.

**

Kenji realized something was amiss when not a single workstation had reported any contacts in four rotations. He decided to start his own little investigation. He reviewed thousands of videos from the cameras hidden in the surveillance room. He worked late into the night through the wee hours of the morning. The results were always the same. Nothing!

He was becoming weary of the long hours and decided this would be his last night. If he found nothing, he would end his quest. He finished his review and froze the video before leaving his console to get a cold drink. He popped the top, turned, leaned against the cabinet, and took a huge gulp. His eyes fixed upon the frozen video frame. On the screen, he watched Jelani stretching with his hands above his head and looking towards the left, his eyes filled with fear. "Not right," Kenji thought.

Lieutenant Kenji started reviewing video from when Jelani was on duty. Five, six rotations ago, Jelani had ended his shift, logged off, picked up his bag and left the room. Starting four rotations back, moments before the end of his shift, he'd started stretching, looking around, and reaching down to his bag. He did not pick up the bag, just reached for it and then logged off his console.

Kenji needed to know what Jelani was up to when he reached for his bag, so he discreetly placed four additional cameras around Jelani's work console. It didn't take long before Kenji witnessed him hiding the memory sphere.

Lieutenant Kenji did not know what information Jelani was smuggling from the surveillance tapes. That was not his responsibility. He did his duty and reported the incident, knowing that investigators would arrive, interview everyone, and settle the matter. He was shocked when Admiral Natan instructed him to place Jelani under house arrest until the investigating team arrived to take custody of him. They were to arrive this very hour.

**

The supply craft was usually unmanned, but today investigators Nalini and Atessa were aboard. Both were new graduates, and this was their first time in deep space.

Nalini sat at the prominent seat of the console, Atessa next to her. The two side by side were an odd pair. Nalini was a petite twenty year old raised in the Marsha mountains high above Lake Vinta. Her skin looked like perfect velvet, with just a touch of green, and her blonde hair was as bright as the sun. Her face was beautiful but there was no mistaking the stern rugged features that exposed her mountain heritage.

In contrast, Atessa towered over her companion by two feet. At first glance, one might mistake her for a brawny cargo handler. But once you got past her massive appearance and came eye-to-eye with her, you would be pleasantly surprised by her gentle demeanor. Born and raised on Ulanitis, the planet of giants, she struggled through her first eighteen years determined to be the first of her family to be accepted into the space academy. She was devastated when she flunked out of flight training, for that was her deepest desire. Now she was content to just be in deep space.

"Nalini, I'm going to dock manually," Atessa bellowed in a manly voice.

"No, you're not. Just leave everything alone and let auto take us in."

"There's no adventure in that," Atessa said. "I've done it before."

Nalini frowned. "No, you haven't."

"I'll bet you four rotations at the Quantronium Spa on Marsha that I can dock without even a bump."

Nalini burst into laughter. "Ya, like you can afford those tickets."

They both settled down and fixed their attention to the live video feed from the many exterior cameras aboard the supply craft. They would be docking soon.

Nalini turned towards Atessa. "Get me a date with your brother, Massimo, and I'll let you dock."

"No problem," Atessa said. She reached and flicked the switch from auto to manual. The craft shot forward at an unprecedented speed and collided with the surveillance modular.

The explosion was horrific.

The distress signals aboard both crafts automatically began sending out location coordinates.

Chapter Fifteen

Rescue One on station above Galvena

"The dining hall is down this corridor." PB Two was hovering, its tracer beam shining down the hallway.

Stone came to an abrupt stop. "Thank you, PB Two." He swiveled like a ballerina and headed in the direction of the beam.

PB Two turned, flew to where the two corridors intersected and hovered to inspect the bulkheads. Inscribed on each corner were directional signs, written in English. Prodigy immediately contacted Dauntless to inform him of the discrepancy.

Dauntless felt the vibration on his wrist. He looked at his computer and read the message from Prodigy. Informational signs written in English are useless, he thought. How in the world did I miss that? Then his mind began racing, reviewing every detail of *Rescue One* to make sure he had not missed any other details. Stone's soft-spoken voice brought him back to reality.

Stone placed his hands on his friend's shoulders. "You look as if you are accountable for all mankind."

Dauntless shook his head. "Sorry, man! That was stupid of me."

Stone headed towards the coffee urn while thinking about how much he loved this new drink. "What do you mean?"

"Writing the signs in English. That's what."

"No need for signs when I have PB Two," Stone shot back. "Where's Nula?"

"Haven't seen her this morning." Dauntless took a huge gulp of orange juice. "I'll figure a way to get those signs fixed."

"I have no doubt, my friend, no doubt at all." Stone was munching on a freshly toasted bagel. I sure do love this Earth food, he thought.

"Nula is finishing her exercises and will join you in a few minutes," PB Two offered.

"Thank you, PB Two," both responded in unison.

Dauntless pushed a stack of computer printout sheet to the center of the table. He placed a tiny vial of liquid on top of the stack.

Stone grabbed the vial and held it to the light to inspect the contents. "An elixir to cure all aliments?" he said, trying to lighten the mood. It didn't work. He realized that Dauntless never stopped working; his mind was always in overdrive. Had to be the energy sphere, he thought.

"It's a tracing liquid you inject into your body."

Stone crossed his arm and took a hard look at his friend. "Really! Why would anyone want to inject tracing fluid into their body?"

Dauntless put his elbow on the table and placed his head in the palm of his hand. "You're working in deep space. Your tether line is severed. You're drifting unnoticed further and further away from the safety of your ship. You are now out of visual sight. Ahh! Prodigy is tracking your location. Saves the day. That's just one of countless scenarios."

"And that, my friend, is why you are in possession of the

sphere."

Nula entered the dining hall and noticed her two loves absorbed in a deep conversation. "Am I missing anything?"

Stone shot to his feet and sent his chair flying across the floor.

Nula tilted her head, smiled at him, and said in her most seductive voice, "Miss me?"

Her brother shook his head and whispered, "Unbelievable."

Stone's face was now glowing bright green. He recovered his composure, retrieved his chair and offered it to Nula. "I'm not sure of the proper greeting. How do you respond on Earth?"

Nula moved closer. "Well, first you say good morning. Then you say how beautiful I look and how my exercise is making me look fantastic. Then you give me a good morning kiss. Simple." She stood on her tiptoes and kissed him on the cheek. "You can stop blushing now."

She left Stone speechless and went to her brother and kissed him on the cheek.

"You're driving the man mad," he whispered to her.

Stone was shaken back to the moment by the vibrating alert tone of his computer. He looked at his wrist, read the alert and sat next to Dauntless. "There's been an accident. The alliance is requesting any craft in the area to respond as quickly as possible. The nearest alliance ship is two rotations away."

"Remind me of what a rotation is?" asked Nula

"Two rotations would be over six Earth days."

The dining hall went silent. They all looked at one another.

"We have to go," Nula said urgently.

"Of course," Stone answered.

"Regardless of the consequences," Dauntless said.

Nula headed for the bridge. "Regardless of the consequences."

**

"Oh, my God!" Nula gasped.

Dauntless was flying manually, inching the huge craft through the expansive debris field. They could see what was left of the surveillance modular far off to their left. There appeared to be a fire still burning. "Probably the oxygen tanks," Stone said.

Dauntless was maneuvering the craft around to the other side, hoping that the blast had sent the debris in one direction. It was slow and tedious.

"What's our plan?" asked Nula.

The bridge was silent. She looked at the two guys. She raised both hands palm up and shrugged her shoulders in disbelief. "Duuu." Still no response from the two. "May I make a few suggestions?"

"Of course," her brother whispered.

She punched him hard in the arm. "Snap out of it," she demanded. "Come on, guys. This is what we trained for. Remember?" she bellowed a bit too loud.

Stone moved to the window and looked out over the disaster. He leaned into the window as if that would jog him into action. "What can the three of us do to clean up that mess? It sure seems different when you see it for real."

"OK, guys, here's what going to happen." Her tone was loaded with authority. "Dauntless, you stay with *Rescue One*.

We might need you to maneuver around once Stone and I are out there."

"Sure, Sis. I'll fly her from bay seven. I can prepare the robot sleds in case we need them."

Nula taking charge had broken the spell.

Stone left his perch on the window and stood looking at Nula with an odd, concerned grin. "You're serious? We're really going out there?"

Nula moved close to him, stretched on her toes and whispered in his ear. "You're going to love it. Besides you'll be with me."

**

It took them a good hour to prepare. Nula was antsy, knowing that every second could make a difference between life and death. But their safety was paramount.

Dauntless recognized his sister's anxiety and reminded her, "Prodigy's censors indicate no life."

Nula kept to her task. "I know, I know, but you can never be sure."

Nula and Stone were geared up and were only minutes away from stepping into deep space.

Nula was checking her list one last time: Robot stretchers; Body bags; Robot sleds; Dissolving restraints; Healing jelly; Debris net; Extra oxygen; Lasers; Cutting and welding torch.

The list was extensive, but Nula was meticulous. When she was satisfied, she gave a thumbs up to Stone and stepped into space. She turned towards Stone and saw him hesitate, hanging onto the hatch. She approached him and held out her hand. "Just step out and grab the line to the sled." Her words were soft and gentle. Nula remembered her first time out and how terrifying it was, but she knew action would overcome fear. She began barking orders to her companion. With each movement, Stone's confidence grew stronger. Before long he had forgotten where he was and concentrated on the task in front of him.

The space walkers moved slowly through the debris using huge inflatable nets to gather the clutter caused by the explosion. Dauntless retrieved the nets and deposited the clutter in the smelting shop. It would be melted, stored and recycled to be used in the three-dimensional printers.

Nula was at the entrance of a large hole blown out of the supply craft. "I'm going inside." She motioned for Stone to come to her. "Tether me to your belt. Can you still see me on your tracker?"

Stone looked at the screen attached to his left arm. "I have both of us," he assured her.

Nula stepped in and waited a moment, looking at the devastation caused by the collision. There was debris floating everywhere.

"Nula!" Stone shouted. "Watch out for sharp shrapnel."

Nula turned and gave him a thumbs up and then motioned for him to join her at the entrance.

They both peered into the craft. Less than five feet from them were what was left of Nalini and Atessa, still strapped into their seats.

"You wait here. I'll go to the sled and get the body bags," Stone said softly.

Nula grabbed his arm. Stone looked into her helmet and saw her crying. "You OK?"

She nodded her head, indicating that she was. "Guess I'm

not so tough."

They touched each other's helmets with an imaginary kiss.

"Don't go in without me. It's going to take both of us to get them free," Stone said sternly.

**

The two astronauts had been working non-stop for five hours. They were both tired. Dauntless was also growing weary, working by himself transporting materials to the smelting shop and resupplying the robot sleds with what his sister needed. The most difficult task was handling the corpses. His friends had sent him thirteen so far. He felt compelled to honor each one somehow. He just didn't know exactly what to do. He transported them to hangar six, carefully laid them on the runway, and then knelt and silently prayed over each one. He vowed to give them a proper ceremony. Nula would know what to do, he thought. He plopped on the floor of hangar six, wiped the sweat from his brow with his arm, took a deep breath, got up, and headed back to hangar seven. "We got to start getting a crew," he said out loud.

**

Nula was moving cautiously around a blown-out hatch leading to what once was the surveillance observation room. She stretched out her arms and held onto the sides of the hatch to catch her breath. The long hours in deep space were beginning to take a toll on her. "We should go back to *Rescue One* and rest for a few hours," she said.

Stone shut the torch off, and turned to see Nula hanging onto the hatch about ten feet from him. His muscles were aching, he was hungry and he had to go to the bathroom. "You tired already?" he said jokingly.

"Dang right I am. It's—" She stopped mid-sentence. She was feeling vibrations in both her hands. "I've got something strange going on over here."

"On my way," Stone said, moving towards her.

The vibrations seem to have a rhythm, like a drumbeat. She released her grip and turned towards Stone. At that instant, the large piece of metal Stone had been cutting broke loose, swiveled, and severed Stone's tether line, then scooped him up and sent him and the line into deep space in the opposite direction from *Rescue One*.

Nula watched in horror as her love disappeared into nothingness. "Stone!" she screamed.

"Nula! Nula!" Stone yelled and Nula could see from his tracker that he was already quite a distance from the crash site. She held on tight to the damaged hatch, trying to control her shaking.

"What is going on?" Dauntless's voice shouted over the radio.

Nula glanced at her oxygen. She had less than one hour remaining. Stone's should be about the same.

"Stone was hit by debris and thrown away from the ship. I'm headed in." She called on every part of her willpower to keep from screaming. "Get the two-man drone ready."

**

Jelani dropped the chair leg he was pounding on the bulkhead with and slithered to the floor, exhausted. He fixed his eyes on his lieutenant laying on the floor, breathing but not moving.

**

Stone had been tossed free from his giant lacrosse stick and was hurtling into space. He gently depressed the control stick to his backpack but it did not respond. He closed his eyes, attempting to gain some control of his equilibrium. He reached into his backpack and slowly turned the relief valve to his oxygen tank. The force of his escaping life blood slowed and eventually stopped his movement. It was then, in the emptiness of space, that he became overwhelmed with his situation. He could feel the panic rise within him like boiling water in a pot.

"Nula! Nula! Do you hear me?"

Silence.

He closed his eyes once again to bring himself back to cadet class and relived the training for this very scenario. He regained his composure and began the memorized checklist. He was satisfied that his suit was still pressurized but dismayed that his computer was smashed. He slowly began a controlled turn, hoping to see *Rescue One*. There was nothing. He was in a world of stars.

He had no way of knowing how much oxygen was remaining and this thought reignited a new bout of terror. He fought through the attack and continued to turn slowly.

He was void of all sense of time, and the silence of space was bizarre, transporting him into a deep state of aloneness. As he turned, a bright pulsating light caught his attention. "Nula! Is that you?"

Overwhelming silence.

"What is wrong with you!" he scolded himself out loud. "Get control of yourself!" he yelled again.

The scolding calmed him down and he was able to collect his thoughts. He began talking out loud and the sound of his voice renewed his determination to stay alive.

He focused on the strange light and was positive that it was moving closer in his direction. "Nula, I knew you would come," he whispered, hoping against all hope it was her.

**

"I've got him on the screen!" Nula yelled from the drone.

"Any communication?" her brother asked. Dauntless had programed the tracer information from Stone's injected serum into the *Rescue One* telescope and was zoomed in on his friend.

"He's rotating slowly," Dauntless relayed to his sister. "He raised his arm. He must be OK."

Nula let out a sigh of relief. "Thank you, God," she said aloud.

Nula switched the lenses of her light beam and turned the ray pink. "I'll be there soon, my love."

**

Stone entered the airlock of the drone. He removed his suit and collapsed to the floor.

Nula waited for the pressure to equalize, rushed in and embraced Stone. They lay entwined on the airlock floor, both crying out of control.

Stone tried to speak but Nula put her finger over his lips

to keep him silent, then kissed him tenderly.

Dauntless yelled, shattering the moment. "Will somebody please tell me what the heck is going on?"

**

Once aboard the mother ship, Dauntless and Stone embraced. "That was a close one, my friend," Dauntless said. He put an arm around Stone's shoulders and they both headed towards the exit to hangar seven.

"Where you guys going?" Nula scolded.

The two male astronauts turned in unison and were shocked to see Nula gearing up for another spacewalk.

Her brother walked over to where Nula was refilling her oxygen tanks. "What are you doing?" He placed his hand on her shoulder and tried to turn her towards him. She pulled away.

"We don't have the luxury of resting," she answered, annoyed. "I don't care if Prodigy's sensors didn't detect life. Someone is alive in that wreckage."

Her brother took a position in front of her. "Come on, Sis, be reasonable. We're all dead tired. We need a rest," he pleaded. "When have you known Prodigy to make a mistake?"

Nula could not be talked down from her mission. She continued to resupply the robot sled. "Fine. You two go do your relaxation thingy ding and help me when you're both nice and refreshed."

Stone gently turned her so that they were face-to-face. He hugged her tight. "Just tell me what you want me to do," he whispered.

Nula stretched her toes to the limit and kissed him on the

check. "Thanks."

"All alliance crafts have multiple airlocks," Stone offered. "We should use the drone and look for one that is not damaged. If we're lucky, we might find a safe way in."

"I'm going with you this time," Dauntless said.

Nula was pacing back and forth like a caged lion. "We should use the four-man drone. That will give us extra room for the survivors." She turned abruptly and headed towards hangar fourteen.

Stone and Dauntless looked at each other. "She takes after my mom," Dauntless offered, a huge grin filling his face. They both followed the alpha.

**

Dauntless maneuvered the drone slowly around the wreckage. Nula and Stone had their eyes glued to their respective monitor screens. Each had different cameras displayed, desperately searching, hoping to find a way into the surveillance station's safe room.

Nula softly punched her brother in the arm. He turned and looked at what she was pointing towards. "Hey, guys, go to camera seven," she instructed.

Below the drone lay an airlock hatch barely visible beneath a collapsed antenna. Dauntless hovered the drone just above the surface.

The drone fell silent. Each of them quietly thought about what to do next. Nula spoke first. "Stone and I should go down and pound on the hatch to see if we can get a response."

**

The two descended towards the hatch, maneuvering gingerly around the downed antenna and positioning themselves into the airlock hatch. Stone raised the steel mallet above his head and with all his strength smashed it against the entrance.

Nula had placed both her hands onto the structure's frame, anticipating a return vibration.

Nothing!

Stone repeated his effort several more times in rapid succession. Nula raised her left hand. "I got something."

Stone pressed the palm of his glove to the top of the hatch. At first the vibrations were rapid, but then they came to an abrupt halt. "What do you think?" he asked.

Nula looked at her companion and could see her reflection in the protective glass of his helmet. "Definitely someone down there. Dauntless, are you copying this?" she asked

"Yes, and filming," he said.

Nula punched her love softly on his arm to get his attention.

"I know. I know." He spoke so softly, as if the sound of his voice would make him miss the vibrations they were both experiencing, which were now coming from the top of the hatch.

They spoke in unison. "Universal code."

"We have a survivor!" Nula shouted to her brother.

"Any idea how we are going to remove that antenna?" Dauntless asked.

Stone cautiously inspected the antenna, moving from one end to the other and checking every detail of the remaining mounting brackets, while Nula tapped out comforting vibrations to the trapped victim.

"Dauntless!" Stone said into his headset. "I think if I tie off the tip of the antenna to the ship's bulkhead cleat and place a small explosive charge to the remaining mounting brackets, it will swing free of the hatch."

"I believe you're right. But I want both of you back in the drone so I can move away before you detonate," Dauntless answered, the last episode still fresh in his mind.

**

All three astronauts were safely in the drone. Dauntless moved the craft away from the collision site. When he felt he was at a safe distance he turned to his friend and gave him a thumbs up. "Go for it."

Stone sent the signal to the detonator. They all watched the antenna fall from its mounting brackets away from the hatch and swing to the far side of the surveillance modular.

"Fly us in, space cadet!" Nula said excitedly.

Her brother hovered over the airlock hatch. All three were looking at the live feed from the drone's cameras. It was obvious the airlocks of both crafts were different.

"That's not good," Stone said.

"It'll be tricky, but we can still go in," Dauntless insisted. "We'll have to work within an argon curtain."

Nula leaned away from her monitor. "If I remember correctly, that will give us less than ten minutes." She sighed a long sigh.

Stone swiveled his chair to face Dauntless. "It's best if I go, as there might be some heavy lifting. We don't know what we're going to find in there."

Nula began to speak but her brother interrupted. "I think

it's best if Nula suits up and goes in. The space is cramped, and I doubt if you and another person will fit in the curtain," Dauntless said to his friend. "You position yourself to assist hoisting the victim into the drone."

Nula sat back and gave her brother a hard look. "Did you consider that there might be more than one survivor? Then what?"

Her brother shrugged. "We'll have to replenish the argon and come back." He put both hands on his head and began to rub his hair. He had a worried look on his face. "Let's go and then we'll deal with whatever we're confronted with."

**

Nula sat at the edge of the drone's airlock. "You have to hold her steady or I'll be toast!" she whispered into her mic.

"I got it. You won't even feel a bump," her brother assured her.

Nula slid off the edge of her perch and into the argon curtain. "Two inches of gas between life and misery," she said softly.

Stone cocked his head, straining to hear. "You say something, Nula?"

She raised her left hand indicating she was OK.

She moved rapidly down the protective curtain and tapped the universal signal indicating it was OK to open the hatch from the other side. She watched as the handle twisted and the hatch fell inward. Instantly, the survivor clawed his way through, manhandling Nula, pushing her towards the argon curtain. She grabbed the side of the exposed airlock to stop herself, inches before breaking the seal of the curtain.

Stone immediately latched onto the survivor's shirt and effortlessly lifted him into the drone. The man, filled with fear, was thrashing about desperately trying to get deeper into the rescue vehicle. Stone grabbed him by his lapels with both hands and forced him into submission. He glanced at his name tag. "Jelani, are there any other survivors?"

He shook his head.

"Nula, he says he's the only survivor. You can get out of there." In his effort to control Jelani, he had not noticed Nula enter the damaged craft.

"He's a liar," she yelled. "I'm with another guy right now." She was cradling an injured survivor's head in her lap. "Send me down some rope. You'll have to haul this guy out of the hatch."

"OK! We'll have to hurry. Time is running out." Stone twisted and removed a set of dissolvable restraints from his bag and bound Jelani's hands and feet. He grabbed his face and forced him to look at him. "When you calm down, they will release." With one quick movement, he rolled to his left, snapped the cabinet latch, grabbed the coiled rope, arched back, and dropped it down the hatch.

Nula tied the rope around the injured man's chest and under both his arms and yelled to Stone, "Start pulling him up slowly."

Nula guided her survivor as her companion hoisted him gingerly out of the damaged craft into the safety of the drone.

Stone placed him on the floor of the drone and looked down the curtain. "Anyone else?" he asked.

Nula looked up through the argon shield. "No one else. Let's get out of here now!"

Stone turned the injured man over, to reveal his

121

identification badge. "Dauntless, we have two new guests. Surveillance Officer Jelani and Lieutenant Kenji.

"Thanks," Dauntless said. "Prodigy already logged their DNA."

Chapter Sixteen

Aboard Rescue One

The three stood somberly silent, their heads lowered. Tears filled Nula's eyes; she did not attempt to wipe them away. Her brother placed his arm around her as if to reassure her that everything would be OK. She knew better.

Stone raised his head. "We should probably say something."

The hangar was engulfed in silence.

"We could say that they died doing what they loved," Dauntless suggested.

Nula raised her head and looked over the thirteen corpses, all in different stages of dismemberment, with all the body parts the astronauts could find lying next to each victim. "We don't know that," she said quietly. "They don't prepare you for this in cadet school." She choked on a sob.

They all hugged, trying to comfort each other.

"I remember some words from when I was an altar boy," Dauntless offered. He stepped forward and stood at the foot of the fallen space workers. He lowered his head. "May the dear Lord accept these children into his home, forgive them their sins and bring them to everlasting life. Amen."

After the service was finished, they loaded the bodies onto a cart and brought them to the morgue where they would be frozen and stored until they could be turned over to the alliance.

"It feels so disrespectful doing this," Nula said.

"It's the only way," Stone assured her. "I'm glad we decided to stay here until the alliance crafts arrive. It will be easier to explain our presence when they witness the work we've done."

Nula started walking ahead of the other two. "I'm going to check on our visitors. Will you guys meet me in the French Riviera in a half hour?"

**

Nula and Stone were wading in the Mediterranean. Dauntless sat at an umbrellaed table, a stack of papers in front of him. He twiddled with a piece of rope. The sun was peeking from behind white fluffy clouds, and a cool refreshing breeze flowed over them, almost making them forget the burial. But none of them could.

Dauntless stood and stretched, and then walked into the sea. He smiled, watching his sister and Stone splash each other playfully. Nula was wearing a pink two-piece bikini and her friend's suit matched perfectly. "You two look like flamingos."

Nula tilted her head, cocked her leg and posed for her brother.

"Is that good or bad?" Stone asked

"PB One, display a video of pink flamingos onto the large screen," Nula ordered.

The screen came alive. All three laughed.

"It feels so good to relax," Nula said, pulling Stone near to her. She glanced at her brother. "What are you working on?" she asked, motioning to the stack of papers piled high on the table.

"Indestructible rope. That fiasco with Stone will never happen again," Dauntless answered.

Nula giggled. "OK, smarty pants. If it's indestructible, how do you cut it?"

"You don't." Dauntless kicked his way out of the water, aiming the spray towards his sister.

He walked to the table and picked up the rope and a small pen-shaped cylinder. He dangled the rope, shook it so they could see it was flexible, and then pressed a button on the side of the pen. A small laser beam appeared and instantly severed the rope. "The laser dissolves the molecules," he said, grinning from ear to ear. "I'm installing one in every suit." He threw the rope remnant on the table and placed the palm of his hand on the stack of papers. "These documents describe and give a solution as to why Prodigy's censors failed to notice life on the wreckage."

Nula and Stone were now standing next to the child prodigy. Nula love-punched him on the arm. "Are you going to keep us in suspense forever or are you going to tell us?"

Dauntless reached for a piece of the wreckage that was hidden amongst the papers. It was smooth and shiny on one side and black and prickly on the other. "This is made from titanium, kamacite and troilite. Prodigy adjusted the censors and solved the problem."

"Wow! You can do all that but you can't figure out how not to burn toast in the morning," Nula snickered. She hugged her brother tightly. "I love you," she whispered in his ear.

PB One flew over to Nula. "Jelani has awakened from sedation and is very agitated."

"Display video on the large screen," Nula requested.

They watched as Jelani paced back and forth within the confines of his room. "Let me out of here!" he was yelling.

Dauntless gave Stone a nod.

Stone knew what his friend wanted. "Prodigy, deploy additional sedative gas into Jelani's cell."

Nula shook her head. "Why do you think he wanted to leave Kenji for dead?"

"Who can say," Stone answered. "We will let the alliance figure that out, but I'm sure it had something to do with the two we found on the supply craft. They were both wearing investigator badges."

Nula walked back into the sea and turned to look at her brother. "I still think we should contact the alliance ships to let them know we're here. They are going to ping us shortly anyway."

"I want us to make first contact," Dauntless answered. "I want them in a defensive position. If Prodigy detects any aggressive movements, he will disable their electronics."

Stone moved closer to his friend. "Command will go on full alert if that happens."

"I expect they will," Dauntless said. He walked into the water until it was above his knees. "Prodigy will restore their communications so that we can explain our presence without the threat of them commandeering *Rescue One*." His voice did not sound confident.

"I hope you're right," Nula responded.

Dauntless shrugged his shoulders and decided to change the subject. "How is our patient?" he asked Nula.

"He's still in a coma. The mechanical spiders I injected probed his entire body and did not detect anything." Nula frowned. "I'm sure a real doctor will be able to help him."

Stone walked into the Mediterranean Sea to join his friends. His computer vibrated. He cocked his wrist and read the message, then sunk to his knees.

Nula and her brother turned to look at him at the same time and found him motionless, a stunned expression on his face.

Nula ran to him, sending water droplets in all directions. "What's wrong?" she said, dropping to her knees in front of him. She could see the sadness in his eyes.

Stone looked into Nula's eyes and forced himself to speak. "There has been a mining explosion on Miranda." A tear slowly trickled down his cheek. "My father is at that mine site." His computer signaled again. "It's my mother. I've got to go. I must talk to her." He stood and left the oasis, PB Two flying over his right shoulder.

Dauntless looked down at his sister still on her knees. "Go with him," he said. "Tell him I am making preparations and we will leave as soon as he is ready."

"What about waiting for the alliance ships?" Nula asked.

"We are not waiting," Dauntless shot back. He turned quickly and walked rapidly towards the exit. "Prodigy, hack the computers in Stone's craft and download all the information." He knew he would need the coordinates for Miranda, and it wouldn't hurt for Prodigy to be in possession of the translating discs.

**

Dauntless had positioned *Rescue One* two hundred and fifty miles above the mining explosion and instructed Prodigy to power the craft and maintain the position. The atmosphere on

Miranda was conducive to supporting life but violent storms were dangerous and frequent. A network of giant domes protected the inhabitants and workers, but the magnitude of the explosion had sent devastating shock waves throughout the compound, breaching a significant number of the protective shields.

The three rescuers were looking at live video from the starboard telescope. It was obvious that the area had been devastated. Dauntless smoothly manipulated the joystick and zoomed into a blown-out section of one of the domes. The scene was total chaos.

The three began talking at the same time and then all stopped together. Nula motioned to her brother. He understood the cue.

"You two go down and get things organized. We know we have many survivors, but Prodigy can't identify which ones need assistance." As he spoke, he began programing all of the spacecrafts aboard *Rescue One* with a tracking device so that they could return to the mother ship without the aid of a pilot.

Nula and Stone stood and began to exit the bridge. Dauntless grabbed his sister's arm. "Wait," he said. They turned towards him. "We will need help. Ask for volunteers. Keep communications open and be safe."

Nula and Stone walked rapidly out of the bridge. Behind them, Dauntless continued to bark instructions to Prodigy. "Activate all bees to assist any visitors. Guest protocol status," they could hear him speaking in a calm voice.

"We should take the transport vessels," Nula said aloud.

"You're right. There will be a large number of people," Stone answered, his voice quivering.

They walked quietly towards the hangars. Stone broke the

silence. "I've never lost anyone close to me before."

Nula could hear the stress in his tone. She stopped quickly, grabbed his arm and forced him to look at her. "You haven't lost anybody. We will find him. I promise. Right now, you've got to get your head on straight. People down there need help and we are their only hope."

**

It was total bedlam on the surface of Miranda. Nula and Stone were desperately searching for someone in charge, but there was no one. At one point, Nula was knocked to the ground and came close to being trampled on. Stone scooped her up and held her tight until the terrified crowd passed.

"This is insanity," she said. She was turning her head in every direction, searching for anyone that even appeared to be trying to help the injured. The throng limited her vision to three feet. She caught site of an observation tower and motioned to Stone. They fought their way through the swarm and climbed to the top of the tower. This vantage point gave them a wide view of the mayhem below.

"Over there," Stone yelled, trying to be heard over the piercing screams of agony and the shrieks of people searching for their loved ones. He grabbed Nula's arm and directed her to look towards an alley to the left of the tower.

In the confusion, they witnessed four individuals moving the injured from the crowded street into the calm of the alley. Without a word, the two rescuers rushed to the alley.

Nula approached one of the good Samaritans and touched his shoulder to get his attention. "Is there anyone in charge?" she asked.

"They are all gone," he said without looking up.

Nula grabbed a handful of bandages and a stapler from her backpack and began to assist. "What do you mean they're gone?" she said, moving to where Stone was injecting a sedative into a crying young woman.

"They're in the mines," he said softly. "No way in." He choked back a sob.

Nula grabbed his arm and tried to turn him, but he pulled away. "There are people alive in the mines?" she yelled to get his attention.

"They can't last much longer. A storm is coming and, with the domes gone, the rest of us will be dead."

Stone reached and grabbed the man forcing him to turn. "How many are trapped?

"I don't know. Maybe fifty. Maybe a hundred. Doesn't matter, they're gone."

"Do you know Zada?" Stone asked, his grip tightening.

The man tried to pull free but Stone would not let him go.

"Zada," Stone shouted. "The potentate of Marsha. He's my father."

The man went limp. "He's in the mine."

Stone released the man. "Do you know if he's alive?"

"I'm not sure."

Stone looked at Nula, then turned and walked down the alley.

Nula offered her hand to the Samaritan. "My name is Nula. We are here to help."

"Help with what? Taking dying people off the street?" he snapped back.

"No!" Nula yelled. "We have a hospital ship orbiting."

"Oh, great," he said. "We can save fifteen or twenty."

Nula's voice softened. "We can save three thousand."

The Samaritan's eyes widened and a smile overtook his gloom. Filled with new hope, he grabbed Nula and hugged her. "My name is Samata," he said.

"Will you help us?" Nula asked.

"Once I spread the word that we can evacuate, we will have all the help we need."

"Can you tell us anything about the people trapped in the mine?" Nula asked.

Samata shook his head. "No, but Loam can."

Loam, hearing his name, came over to join the conversation.

"Will you take me to the mine?" she asked Loam. He nodded.

Nula walked over to where Stone was leaning against a steel beam. He was throwing up. She leaned against his back and wrapped her hands around his waist. "Are you going to be OK, or do you need to go back to the ship?"

He raised his head, inhaled deeply and exhaled slowly. "I'll be fine. Give me a few minutes."

"Will you work with Samata and get the evacuation under way? I'll go with Loam to the mine and then send him back for you." She handed him a roll of gauze so he could wipe his face.

Stone stood tall, wiped his face and looked at Nula. "Find a way to get them out," he pleaded.

"I promise," she said, knowing the promise was impossible.

Loam held her arm and the two scurried off.

**

131

When Nula and Loam arrived at the mine, they found an organized rescue effort under way. They quickly found the man in charge. A massive individual, his face was blackened and his clothing shredded, with cut wounds on his arms, legs and face. Most were still bleeding. He was throwing huge rocks off of a piece of equipment as if they were cotton balls.

"Sir," Nula shouted over the buzz and clanking of machinery.

He turned and looked at her. His eyes were white and glared through the soot on his face like two beacons. His towering demeanor was intimidating but when he spoke his voice was soft and gentle. Not what Nula had expected from this giant.

"Be careful, little girl. There's a lot of sharp metal sticking up from these rocks."

Nula held her hand out in friendship. "My name is Nula and I'm here to help."

The giant smiled and then burst into laughter so loud that the other rescuers stopped what they were doing to see what was so funny during this moment of tragedy.

The giant held out his bloody hand. "I'm Panova," he said, recognizing the angry look on Nula's face. "I'm sorry, but I have been pleading for volunteers for a long time, and they sent you for this work." He waved his hand over the debris field. "No work for a little girl."

Nula could feel her anger swelling within her and fought to control the beast. She punched Panova hard. "PB One, lock my position," she instructed. "Dauntless, do you have me?"

Aboard *Rescue One,* Dauntless was frantically entering his sister's coordinates into the telescope's computer. "I got you, Sis."

"Melt some rock for me." She took a small laser from her bag and shot a thin green beam onto the rocks a safe distance away from the workers. Instantly a red laser beam pierced through the darkened sky and silently turned the boulders into a red stream of lava. "I'm here to help," she repeated. "Will you please tell me where you think the survivors are located?" Nula said, her voice soft.

Panova and the others stared in disbelief. The giant held his hands in a calming manner. "OK."

"Nula," she said. "My name is Nula.

"OK, Nula let's go over there where it's not so noisy.

**

Nula cleaned and bandaged Panova's wounds while telling him about the evacuation of the injured to *Rescue One*.

"I can't believe Zada's boy is here. I haven't seen him since the start of mining on Usra." Nula had cleaned the giant's face, revealing rugged and stern features. But his voice exposed his gentleness. "There are five shafts," he continued, pointing to a mangled and dirty map. "Nearest we can tell, they were all inspecting shaft three."

Nula interrupted. "PB One, scan the map and send it to Dauntless."

PB One completed the task and hovered over Nula's shoulder.

Panova watched, bewildered.

Dauntless's voice bellowed through PB One's tiny speakers and into Nula's ear bud. "The censors show life about one mile below the surface. Give me a second." Her brother was fine-tuning Prodigy's information. "I got a number of contacts. About fifty, I estimate."

Nula looked at Panova. "That's them. Any ideas?"

Panova waved his arm in the direction of a huge piece of equipment. "We can get ninety-nine per cent of the way with the tunneler but it won't start, and all the mechanics are dead."

Nula rushed over to the massive rock eating monster and started opening hatches and panel covers. PB One hovered over each and transmitted the information to Dauntless.

"You got two dead batteries," he said. "Have PB One land on each one and Prodigy will send an electrical charge. That ought to do it."

"Any word from Stone?"

"He's OK, Sis. He's busy with the evacuation. He's brought six hundred and twelve aboard so far."

"Tell him I think I might have found his father." She was quiet for a moment. "Maybe you shouldn't. I don't want to give him false hope."

**

Panova guided the rock-eating monster deeper and deeper into the ground. There was only room for one in the enormous piece of equipment and the giant filled the seat. Nula squeezed next to him against his objections. What a comical sight, she thought: a giant with his armed wrapped around a doll with a bee on her shoulder.

Behind the rock crusher, a number of workers were frantically cleaning the debris and constructing haphazard shoring. There was no time to do it right. They all accepted that they were putting their lives at risk.

Dauntless used his sister's tracking implant to guide the two rescuers within two feet of the trapped entourage. "I don't think you should go any further using the tunneler," he warned.

Panova and Nula climbed out of the upper hatch and stood on the roof of the equipment.

"PB One, use your laser and burn through the remaining rock," Nula instructed.

The robot bee was able to create a tiny opening big enough for it to fly through.

"I've got video!" Dauntless yelled.

Nula jumped in the air and grabbed Panova around the neck. "We got them," she shouted over the roar of the rock gobbler.

Panova picked her up, held her high and kissed her. His lips covered most of her face.

People on both sides desperately clawed at the rocks until the space was big enough for Nula to fit through. She entered the cramped chamber and was immediately overwhelmed with the smell of vomit, urine and death.

"Is Zada here?" she yelled.

"I'm over here," he shouted.

Nula grabbed one of the rattled survivors and forced him to look at her. "Crawl through and do exactly what the man on the other side tells you. His name is Panova. Do you understand?"

The man was shaking rapidly but answered, "Yes."

She went over to Zada. "I'm Nula," she said, taking bandages from her pouch.

"How do you know me?"

"Your son brought us here."

Zada shook his head in disbelief. "That's not possible."

Nula shrugged. "Yet here we are. Can you walk?" She grabbed him under his arms and assisted him to his feet.

"Where is my son?" he demanded.

"He is evacuating everyone," she answered, moving him along to the escape portal.

Zada planted his feet. "Evacuating? I don't understand."

Nula yanked him forward. "Most of the domes have been compromised. It's a long story and we don't have time for it now," she said sternly.

Zada would not move. "I'm staying until everyone is safe."

"Like hell you are," Nula scolded. "I promised your son I would get you out and that's what I intend to do." She yanked him again. He relented.

**

All the survivors were free. Nula yelled out to Panova, "I'm going to make one last check."

"We don't have time to remove the dead. We have to go now," Panova shouted back.

"I want to make sure we don't leave anyone alive," she shrieked.

She moved from one corpse to another, checking for vital signs. She heard the faint explosion, felt the distant rumble, cocked her head, and looked up as the chamber ceiling crashed upon her.

When the giant peered through the hole, Nula was gone.

Chapter Seventeen

Aboard *Rescue One*

The space reeked of medicine. The two rescuers' nostrils quivered as they entered the operating room. They walked slowly; Dauntless sobbed uncontrollably. When they reached Nula, he fell to his knees. "It's all my fault," he managed to say between choking sobs. "I'm so damned arrogant. She was so afraid but I promised I would take care of her. She trusted me, looked up to me. How stupid am I to think I could keep her safe?"

Nula lay broken, her face awkwardly distorted. Her left eye was black, there was no right eye. Dauntless placed a hand on his sister's head. Her once soft tan skin was cold and brittle. His tears fell onto exposed bones. Her legs and arms were crushed.

Nula's body was suspended in mid-air. There was a semicircle of monitors from mid-wall to ceiling displaying information sent from the twenty medical spiders that had been injected into her. Prodigy captured the information, calculated the success of survival and programed the cloning machines to give priority to the patients with the greatest chance of recovery. There were hundreds of requests and Nula's status was the lowest.

Stone stood behind his friend and placed his hands on his shoulders. "You can't blame yourself," he said. "She would not want that. You saw how much she loved being part of your dreams." He could feel Dauntless's body shudder, unable to control his sorrow. "She wanted to make a difference and she did. She might have started afraid but she is the bravest person I've ever known. She saved you. She saved me, my father and countless others. We could live forever and not accomplish what she has."

Dauntless shook his head violently. "No!" he sobbed. "This is my fault." He flicked his thumb, exposing the glow star. He threw it against the wall. He did not care that its brilliance was fading. It went black.

Stone felt his sorrow swelling and knew he would need every ounce of willpower to prevent his emotions from exploding. He must control himself for the sake of his friend. But how could he keep himself together while his beautiful Nula lay dying as he stood by, useless. He offered his own life to the Great One in place of hers. His prayer was not rewarded.

"But she's not gone yet. She hasn't given up and neither will we," he said softly.

Stone noticed it first. Nula's left pinky finger lifted from the table. He leaned to her and placed his hand on hers. It lifted again. "We are here, Nula," he whispered in her ear. "We will never leave you." Her pinky moved and her lips parted.

Dauntless, now aware of what was happening, got up and moved to the other side. He held her arm with both hands. His sister's pinky moved rapidly up and down. He lowered his head close to her lips. "Mom," she said so softly that it was difficult to understand. He kissed her tenderly on her forehead.

"I'll get you home. I promise," he said.

Stone looked at his friend. "Did she say something?"

"She said, 'Mom'. She must be thinking of Mom and

Dad."

Nula's pinky lifted again but this time she did not lower it. Her brother leaned towards her once again. "Mom," she repeated.

Dauntless's head shot up. "Oh, my God! You were always the smart one." He grabbed his confused friend's arm and pulled him towards the door. "Come on, we have no time to waste." He stopped abruptly at the entrance. He turned and looked at his sister. "Prodigy, play 'Runaway'.

PB One flew over to the glow star on the floor. It hovered over it, opened a compartment in its hull and sucked it up. It then flew over to Nula and deposited the glow star onto her left shoulder. It instantly glowed brighter than ever before. Its new master slowly tilted her head so that the glow engulfed her. Nula's distorted face forced a smile.

Chapter Eighteen

Aboard *Rescue One*

Surveillance Officer Jelani awoke from his sedative induced sleep. He could see many people rushing up and down the hall outside his room. He walked over to the open door and slowly peered out into the buzz of activity. Where did all these people come from, he thought. He entered the corridor and walked slowly down the hall, looking into each open door. He recalled being escorted down this same hallway and all the doors were closed then. He stopped a beautiful young lady walking next to a hovering stretcher. The patient on the legless gurney was smiling and praising her for helping him escape.

"What's going on?" Jelani asked. "What is he talking about?" He motioned to the fellow on the stretcher.

The young lady looked at Jelani in disbelief. "Where have you been?" she said, mocking him.

"I've been sedated. Why are all the doors opened?" Jelani asked. His gaze fixed on the small mechanical robot flying over the lady's right shoulder.

The young lady looked down at the floor, ashamed of her sarcastic comment. "Please forgive me, my sir. There was a mining explosion on Miranda. This ship evacuated thousands from the surface. Everyone who can is helping the injured. The captain of this vessel ordered all the doors opened so that it would be easier for us to find a place to put the injured. We are really cramped for room."

Jelani pointed towards his room. "That one is empty," he offered.

"Bless you, my sir," the young lady said, moving towards the room. "You should find some place to sit securely. The captain announced that we would be entering dimensional speed in fifteen minutes. Whatever that is."

Jelani froze in disbelief. "I knew it," he said aloud.

"May I be off assistance?"

Jelani turned to find a mechanical robot hovering at eye level. "Who. No, what are you?"

"I am PB One-five-one and will direct you to where you wish to go."

"Do you have any shuttles? I wish to leave this ship," Jelani demanded.

PB One-five-one positioned itself over Jelani's right shoulder and shot a laser beam down the hallway. "Please proceed down this corridor, stop at the yellow sign and take the elevator to level one. You will find what you are looking for there."

Jelani walked briskly towards the yellow sign, glancing in each room. He passed room two-nine-nine-one, stopped suddenly, then took a step backwards. The room was packed with injured people, amongst them was Lieutenant Kenji. He studied the room. No one was moving. He walked over to his boss's bed. Kenji looked at Jelani. "I know what you did," he whispered in a feeble voice.

Jelani's neck twitched. *I left you to die,* he thought.

Jelani could feel his heart racing, and the twitching of his neck was becoming violent. He looked around the room and, when he was confident that no one was awake, he took a pillow and smothered his boss until his life was gone.

He exited room two-nine-nine-one and ran to the elevator. He arrived at the hangar bays and was confronted with an array of different spacecrafts. He moved quickly about and choose a smaller passenger craft. He called upon all his computer skills to gain entry. Once inside, he hacked into the craft's computer and found the protocol code. He entered it into the flight recorder: XTFGTR453. Prodigy recognized the code that Dauntless had given Stone and opened the outer bay doors, exposing deep space. Jelani flew out from *Rescue One* in Stone's spaceship and was out of view in seconds.

Chapter Nineteen

Aboard *Rescue One*: control room

It was taking Dauntless and Stone longer to prepare *Rescue One* for its upcoming journey, so much so that Dauntless was becoming annoyed. His thoughts were nagging at him. *My sister's life depends on getting started quickly. She doesn't have much time left. The very people whose lives she saved are causing the delays. How ironic.*

Dauntless's attention was drawn to the monitor displaying portions of the flight bays. An amber light flashed continually, indicating an airlock was opened. *What now?* He watched in disbelief as Stone's spacecraft left *Rescue One*.

"Prodigy. What's going on in bay fifteen?" Dauntless demanded.

Stone overheard his friend and came to stand beside him.

Prodigy responded instantly. "I received proper protocol from Stone's spacecraft and cleared him for departure."

"Play video," Stone demanded. He looked at his friend. "What just happened?"

"Zada is requesting permission to enter the bridge," Prodigy informed the captain. "I am displaying video of bay fifteen," Prodigy continued.

Stone looked at Dauntless and they both shrugged. "This can't be good," Stone said. "Prodigy, permission for Zada to enter."

Zada stepped onto the bridge and, even though he was in awe at the magnificence of the control room, he controlled his emotions and gave no hint of his wonderment. He moved quickly to where his son and Dauntless were both hunched over a monitor.

The two friends watched as Jelani entered Stone's spaceship and rocketed off in *Rescue One*. "Prodigy, back track Jelani from his quarters and display the video. Can you believe this guy?" he said to Dauntless.

Zada moved closer to his son and asked in a low voice, "Can I talk to you for a moment?" He was also looking at the displayed video. "Did he just kill that man?" he said in astonishment.

The three looked at one another. Dauntless broke the silence. "I don't have time for any distractions. Pass the word we're departing in ten minutes," he demanded urgently.

Stone held his father's arm and guided him off to the side out of hearing distance from his friend.

Zada turned towards his son. "What is going on here? What is this ship?"

Stone held his hand up, hoping it would stop the questions flowing from his dad. It was no use.

Zada continued with his questions. "You cannot allow that man to escape after we witnessed him killing someone."

"Father, please be silent so I can explain," Stone said shyly. He had never talked to his father this way before. "Our mission is more important."

Zada began to speak but Stone motioned for him to stop.

Stone drew in a deep breath and exhaled slowly. "Do you remember the girl who just saved your life in the mine?" Zada indicated that he did. "She's dying and the only way to save her is to take her to Earth."

Zada shook his head repeatedly. "No! That's impossible. Earth is a restricted planet. I forbid it," he said, exerting his authority.

Stone looked at the ceiling and drew in another deep breath. He met his father's angry eyes. "I'm sorry, Father, but for the second time in my life I must disobey you. I'll explain everything when we complete the mission."

Zada was not finished. "I want to speak to the captain, now," he demanded.

Stone placed his hand on his father's shoulder. "I am the captain."

Zada's shoulders collapsed. "How can that be possible?"

"Father, time is of the essence. I beg you to sit with us." Stone motioned his father to the flight chair next to the captain's command seat. "I pledge I will explain everything to you after our journey. If then you believe that the alliance will not sanction our mission goals, I will relinquish this magnificent craft to their command."

Dauntless finished his preparations and returned to the control seating area. He looked at his friend and his father, seated in anticipation of the journey. His eyes fixed on Zada. He bowed his head in respect. "Please forgive me for my rudeness. These are trying times. This is not how I envisioned our first meeting."

Zada placed a closed fist to his chest and then extended it towards Dauntless, as a gesture of respect and understanding. He turned and looked at his son. "Are we still above Miranda?"

"Yes. About eight hundred miles off the surface," Stone answered.

Zada cocked his head as if calculating a problem. "If my memory is correct, Earth is about twelve rotations away. Will your sister survive such a trip?" he asked Dauntless.

Dauntless turned and looked at Zada. He smiled for the first time since seeing his sister's broken body. "This ship can make the trip in less than twenty minutes Earth time."

Zada sat motionless, looking dumbfounded.

Stone leaned over to his father and whispered, "I have so many things to tell you."

Zada shook his head slightly, freeing himself from his disbelief. "Where are the interplanetary coma masks?"

Stone placed his hand on his father's shoulder. "We don't need them. Like I said, I have so many surprises for you."

"Thirty seconds and counting." Dauntless looked at Stone. "By the way I had Prodigy fry the propulsion guidance system to your spacecraft. Jelani's craft is dead in the middle of nothingness."

Prodigy finished the countdown. "Five-four-three-two-one." *Rescue One* disappeared.

Chapter Twenty
Voyage to Earth

Stone positioned *Rescue One* on the dark side of Earth's moon with just the bridge sneaking a view of the magnificent planet. He instructed Prodigy to hold the position. He looked towards his father and then to Dauntless who gave him a slight nod. "Father, I must beg your forgiveness but I must request that you leave the bridge."

Zada gazed at his son in bewilderment.

"Father, it is best that you have no knowledge of what is about to occur," Stone said, making every effort to keep his tone respectful.

Zada fought back the urge to reprimand his son. "I have already voiced my disapproval. It's obvious my opinion is not welcomed." He turned abruptly and headed towards the exit.

"Zada, my I have a word with you? Please," Dauntless asked.

Zada stopped and turned to look at Dauntless.

Dauntless moved close and spoke softly to Zada. "May I ask you to do me a tremendous favor?" Dauntless held both his hands together as if praying.

Zada recognized the sadness in Dauntless's eyes and tenderness in his voice. He lowered his head in respect. "I will do whatever you request."

Dauntless smiled. "PB Two will take you to my sister.

Will you prepare her for her trip to the surface? I ask that you bring her to bay thirty-six when you are ready. PB Two will show you the way."

Zada nodded in agreement and then exited the bridge with PB Two flying over his shoulder.

Dauntless turned and walked to his friend's side and placed a hand on his shoulder. "He will come to understand once we explain everything."

Stone stood erect. "I hope so. I hate feeling he is disappointed with me." He shook his head to clear his mind. "Tell me your plan. You do have one, I hope?"

Dauntless guided his friend to the hologram maps. "I wanted to land on Broken Bone Hill but my dad said that there are federal agents all over the place."

Stone placed a hand on his friend's shoulder. "It's probably best we don't go there, anyway. You don't want your parents to see Nula injured," he said.

"You're right," Dauntless answered. "Anyway, I chose this spot." He pointed to a dot on the map. The map expanded to reveal Palmerston Island. "It's the most isolated island on Earth. It sits in the Pacific Ocean hundreds of miles from its nearest neighbor."

Stone rubbed the top of his head with both his hands. "So many things can go wrong," he said apprehensively.

"That's true. We will take the four-man drone. Once on the ground, PB One and PB Two will monitor all electronic signals. If we're in danger of being detected, Prodigy will disable the threat. I developed the technology that most of my world is using and created a back door to the programs. I hope I don't have to use it."

Stone nodded in agreement. "What's your plan once we're

back on board?" he asked as they both walked side by side to exit the bridge.

"There's over a thousand injured aboard. I was thinking about transporting them to hospitals on Earth," Dauntless said while walking.

Stone stopped abruptly and turned to face his colleague. "That, my friend, would start a series of events that we could not control. My father is the newly elected potentate of Marsha and is now missing along with thousands of the population of Miranda. The alliance is searching for them as we speak."

Dauntless recognized the concern and stress in his friend's voice. "What do you recommend?" he asked.

**

Zada gasped in horror at the sight of Nula's broken body suspended in mid-air, the glow star drenching her in soft comforting rays. He moved slowly to her side, and his thoughts went back to when this angel had entered the mine chamber ready to rescue everyone. He wept freely as he realized this beautiful, vibrant young girl was willing to sacrifice her life to save his. He felt ashamed. Would he be brave enough to do the same if the situation was reversed?

"I requested a robot stretcher," PB Two offered.

Zada walked completely around Nula. "How do I move her?"

PB One flew over to Zada and hovered in front of him at eye level. "When the stretcher arrives, I will position it beneath her and then release her from suspended animation."

"Is there anything I can cover her with?" Zada asked.

PB Two hovered in front of a white cabinet. "In here."

Zada removed a pure white sheet and draped it over Nula. He leaned over and kissed her gently on her blackened forehead. When he raised his head, he noticed Nula's lips had parted. He lowered his head and strained to hear what she was saying. "Thank you," she whispered as she raised her pinky finger. Zada saw the movement and tenderly held her hand. Nula's one eye was open wide and her lips tried to form words. After a few moments and with great effort, Nula managed to whisper, "I am so glad you're safe."

Zada fell to his knees and wept bitterly. He felt angry with himself for not insisting that he stay in the mine chamber instead of her.

The robot stretcher arrived and Nula was placed onto it. Zada followed PB One and PB Two down the corridor leading to bay thirty-six. His hand rested on Nula's broken arm. As he walked, he understood why his son would be willing to risk everything to save this remarkable Earthling.

**

Dauntless and Stone continued to walk in silence. They reached bay thirty-six and stood quietly watching Zada and Nula coming towards them from the opposite direction. The sight of her on the robot gurney reignited a deep sadness within both of them. Stone spoke softly. "Let's finish as quickly as possible, then head to Galvena. We can orbit there safely. I think we should talk to my father before we continue with any new plans."

Dauntless fought to control his emotions. "Of course," he said, fighting back his sorrow.

They both remained quiet with their own thoughts. Stone

was longing for his beautiful Nula to be whole again. Dauntless was angry with himself and feeling responsible for his sister's condition. His spirts brightened slightly when he noticed the shine from the glow star emanating from beneath the sheet draped over Nula. It meant she was gaining strength.

The three men moved Nula from the robot into the drone.

"Thanks, Father," Stone said. "We will take her from here."

"I am coming with you," Zada said firmly.

Stone was about to object but stopped when Dauntless grabbed his arm. "It's OK," Dauntless assured his friend.

**

The phenomena began as soon as the drone entered Earth's atmosphere. Stone's and Zada's hands began glowing brightly. The radiance from the glow star and glowing hands flooded the craft with a warm comforting sensation.

Dauntless chose the remotest section of the island. PB One and PB Two were deployed to check the area.

Together, Stone and Zada placed their glowing hands gently onto Nula's battered body. The three watched in wonderment as Nula's body began to heal. First, her black and blue bruises disappeared, then her shattered exposed bones folded back into her body, her missing eye appeared, and her skin became tanned and soft as velvet.

Each of the men was engulfed in his own thoughts. Dauntless and Stone relived the moment Marian, Dauntless's Mom, was healed ten years ago in a small hospital in Saratoga Springs, New York. Zada was in awe at witnessing this miracle for the first time and remembering his son's questions about why the alliance would be against this healing power and restrict travel to this magnificent planet. No one spoke. All three were crying.

Nula opened her eyes, stretched both arms above her head, let out a soft groan and said, "Hi, guys." She looked down, saw she was naked and pulled the sheet tight around her body. "Oops."

Dauntless stood and walked to the back of the drone and returned with clothes for his sister.

"Thanks, Kevin. Oh, sorry, I mean Dauntless," she said, embarrassed.

Dauntless touched her tenderly on her cheek. "That's OK. Call me whatever you want. You know, you look just like Mom," he said, bringing a smile to her face.

The three men walked to the opposite side of the drone to allow Nula to dress in private.

Zada placed a hand on his son's and Dauntless's shoulders. "This was the right thing to do," he said quietly. Both boys nodded in agreement.

Nula came up behind Stone, startling him. She grabbed his face with both hands and kissed him long and passionately. "I love you."

Stone swallowed his sobs, took a few seconds to compose himself and then answered, "I love you dearly." Then he began to cry. Nula held him close.

Dauntless moved behind his sister and put his arms around her and Stone. She reached behind her and placed the palm of her right hand against his cheek. The three remained entwined until they were comforted.

Nula broke the embrace and turned to Zada. "I am so happy you are here," she said.

Zada moved close to her and placed his forehead onto hers. "I am honored to be in your presence," he whispered in her ear. He lifted his head and gazed into her eyes. "You are truly Nula."

Nula stepped over to her brother and love-punched him in the arm. "Can we get out of here. I'm starrrrving."

They all laughed.

When they were all seated and prepared for the return to *Rescue One*, Nula held the glow star and offered it to her brother. "You are the only one pure enough to unlock its secrets."

Dauntless accepted the gift and placed it in his thumb with a flick.

Chapter Twenty-One

Aboard *Rescue One*: French Riviera

Dauntless, Stone and Nula walked together towards the elevator. Nula was sandwiched between the boys and holding onto her brother's right arm and Stone's left arm. They were all wearing bathing suits. Of course, Nula's and Stone's suits were matching pink. PB One was flying slightly behind Nula. She had placed her sliver of the glow star into her robot the night before: now its radiance was reflecting off the atomic diamond battery through the camera lenses drenching her in a kaleidoscope of soft pink rays.

There were many people in the corridor, all of them going to the French Riviera. A line was formed in front of the elevator doors. As the crowd noticed the three leaders, they would stop and stand against the bulkhead, heads bowed. The people in line at the elevator parted, allowing them to pass. They also stood against the bulkhead and bowed their heads.

"What are they doing?" Nula asked.

"I have no idea," Stone said, turning away from his love so she wouldn't see his mischievous grin.

They entered the empty elevator and Nula motioned for others to join them but no one made any attempt to enter. "What in the world is going on? Is there something wrong with us?" She gave her brother a puzzled glance. He shrugged and pressed the button that would send them quickly to level fifteen. The doors opened and Nula was amazed at the hundreds of people on the beach or in the Mediterranean. She pulled her brother's arm and tugged him close. "This is precisely how I envisioned our guests relaxing and having a good time," she said. She noticed the fantastic sights of space flashing by on the big movie screen. "What's that?" she asked her brother as the planet Pluto came into view and flashed by.

"Isn't it beautiful?" Dauntless said. "Prodigy solved the mystery of the lost video from our voyage."

The three gazed at the screen along with the multitude of beach visitors. The screen would turn black for a moment and then in the distance the Black Eye Galaxy would speed towards them and flash past the cameras of *Rescue One*. Blackness of space again, but then seconds later NGC 1275, the heart of the Perseus Cluster, came into view. With the galactic collision still in view they could identify the Antennae galaxies less than ten million light years away. For many at the beach, it was the first time they had witnessed their home galaxy from this perspective.

"Nula!" a voice shouted from down the beach.

Nula turned to see who was calling her. She let go of her brother's arm and waved towards the direction of the voice. To her amazement, everyone in the French Riviera turned and tried to position themselves to get a glimpse of their goddess.

The movie screen went dark. The sun and clouds disappeared and the ceiling panels to the top level of *Rescue One* parted, exposing a billion sparkling stars. The large screen exploded with live video of Nula. PB One was hovering just behind her and showering her with soft pink rays resembling a halo. Everyone gasped.

"What's going on?" Nula demanded.

She turned to exit but Stone leaned towards her and whispered, "You have to stay. They want to thank you and show their respect."

"Thank me for what?" Nula said softly. She glanced at the big screen and choked back her emotions when she saw herself with PB One behind her. "PB One, land here," she said, placing her hand on her right shoulder. PB One obeyed but the result was not what Nula expected. The glow now bounced off her diamond earring, where she had encapsulated the translation node, sending pink rays that seemed to originate from her upper torso. "Oh, my God!" She inhaled and placed both her hands over her mouth.

Zada was the first to approach with both his hands extended. She quickly grabbed and squeezed them. "This is so unnecessary," she said.

"No, my child. These people are in pain. They have lost everything. They truly need this experience." He stood next to her. "I'll stay by your side."

Tears filled Nula's eyes. Her brother offered a towel. She glared at him. "I just wanted to swim and relax," she hissed.

The crowd was mulling about and lines started forming along the beach.

"What are they doing?" Nula asked Zada.

"They are separating according to their planet of origin," Zada answered.

First came the Marshians; one by one they stood in front of Nula, held a closed fist to their breast and slowly extended it towards her. Each placed a possession they had managed to bring with them from Miranda at her feet. Nula looked each one in the eye and, fighting to control her emotions, she simply said, "Thank you."

People of the Ulanites knelt on one knee, touched her sandal, left their gift and quickly moved on.

The Knobanies held their hands up, palms facing Nula for a moment and then deposited their gift.

Zada touched Nula's arm. "They want to share your aura," he whispered.

Last in line was the giant Panova. He stood before her; his clothing was shredded, bruises lined his arms and legs, but he was grinning hugely. "I have no gift for you."

Nula could take no more. She burst into tears and ran to the giant and attempted to put her arms around his massive torso. Panova picked her up as if she was a feather. He placed her on his shoulders. "Enough of this sadness," he bellowed. He headed towards the ocean with Nula still riding on his shoulders. "Let's have some fun!" He ran to the deepest part of the Mediterranean and still hoisting Nula, he dove into the sea. When he and Nula surfaced, they found that hundreds had joined them. In the water, she could put her arms around the giant's neck. "Thank you, my hero."

The giant extended his huge hands over the throng of people in the water.

"It is we who thank you," he yelled as loud as he could.

The crowd chanted, "Nula! Nula!"

Nula threw them a kiss and yelled, "I love you all."

Then the party began.

**

Nula, Dauntless and Stone moved amongst the beach goers, laughing and enjoying their stories while forming bonds of friendship. There were many robot gurneys holding injured patients. These survivors had not been able to present themselves to Nula earlier. Nula took a moment with each one, holding their hand or kissing their cheeks. The three approached a beautiful young girl whose left leg had been crushed. She was sitting up with her injured leg in a cast and resting on a shelf extending from the robot stretcher.

Nula held her left hand. The girl lowered her head. "I never met an Earthling before. Are they all goddesses?"

Nula touched the girl's chin and gently lifted her head. Their eyes met and Nula gasped in disbelief: the girl's irises were an enchanting pink. "No one on Earth is a goddess. What's your name?"

The girl spoke in a whisper, "Chununa."

"You have the most beautiful eyes that I have ever seen. Where are you from?" Nula asked.

Chununa's demeanor changed. She smiled broadly. "Veinites," she answered enthusiastically.

Nula lifted the girl's hand and kissed it. "That's a wonderful name. I imagine it is as gorgeous as you."

A tiny tear formed in the corner of Chununa's eye, then trickled down her velvet cheek. "I am ashamed that I have no gift for you. I was rescued from Miranda with just these ragged clothes."

Nula embraced her. "Your presence here is the most precious gift."

Nula stood up and walked over to her brother who was looking over the hundreds of people clustered in the sea or gathered under beach umbrellas. She stood behind him and put her arms around his waist. "Amazing, isn't it? Aren't you glad I was so persnickety with every detail?"

Her brother continued to scan the entire French Riviera.

"It is fantastic, Sis. Look around and tell me what you see."

Nula released him and stood at his side while she scanned the crowd. "People having fun, relaxing and enjoying one another."

Dauntless pointed to a cafe. "Look over there. That guy is serving food. Why? Who prepared it?" He then pointed down the beach towards a small group of people picking up trash and placing it in a robot dumpster. "How did they know where the robot was, not to mention how it worked?" He turned and looked at his sister. "That's what I find amazing."

Nula called to Stone and waved for him to come over. She felt excited just watching him walk towards her. *God, I love him so much,* she thought.

When he got to Nula, he kissed her tenderly.

"Really?" Dauntless said.

Nula punched her brother while still in Stone's embrace.

After Dauntless pointed out to his friend what he had shown his sister, he asked. "Who organized these people? And what motivation do they have?"

"Ahh, I kind of did," Stone admitted.

Nula and Dauntless looked at their friend with raised eyebrows.

"I asked Prodigy to send all the robot bees out and about to interview all our guests. Once we found out what jobs they had on Miranda, it was easy for Prodigy to assign them tasks. We discovered that most have a diversity of skills."

"But why would they agree to work?" asked Nula.

Stone fidgeted. "Most everyone was so grateful. Ahhh, you know what I mean."

Nula and Dauntless looked at their friend, tilted their heads and scrunched their eyes, recognizing the fib.

Stone rocked from side to side. "Well, ahh, umm," he stammered. "I told them you would take care of them when we arrive at Marsha."

Dauntless crossed his arm in front of his chest. "And how am I going to do that?"

Stone put both his hands out, palms up, and shrugged his shoulders, indicating he had no idea.

**

Zada found his way over to where the three were siting. "We should talk," he said.

The trio nodded. "Give us ten minutes to change and then we'll all meet on the bridge," Nula suggested.

"Very well," Zada said as he turned and headed towards the exit with PB Three flying over his right shoulder.

Dauntless looked at Stone and smiled. "He seems more relaxed."

Stone drew in a deep breath and exhaled slowly. "He told me he was going to contact a colleague in the alliance. The conversation must have gone well."

Nula got up and stood behind Stone. She put her arms around his neck and placed her cheek on the top of his head. The glow from PB One lit his face in a pink glow. She squeezed him closely. "I'll meet you on the bridge." She released her grip, turned and left the French Riviera. Stone watched googly-eyed until she disappeared.

Dauntless looked at his friend. "You two have it bad," he said, shaking his head.

"What?" Stone asked.

Dauntless stood from the table. "Never mind. Let's go."

**

When Nula arrived on the bridge, Zada was already seated at a large round table built from a single piece of red wood. As she approached, she could see Zada's reflection in its lacquered finish. The table had no visible means of support but when Nula leaned on it to greet Zada, it did not move.

The potentate of Marsha pushed his chair back to stand but Nula touched his hand to stop him. "Please, my sir, continue to enjoy the view."

Zada offered her the chair next to his. "Isn't it astonishing?"

The conference table sat on a section of the control room that was cantilevered over the side of *Rescue One*. The floor, ceiling and walls were manufactured from a solid piece of glass. The two sat in silence and gazed at the spectacular panorama of stars.

Zada spoke while still staring into space. "I want to thank you and your brother for your gifts. I believe Dauntless is correct. The graphene and graphite carbon nanotubes will solve the weight and strength problems that arose during the construction of our new space station." He turned and looked at Nula. "How did he know they were having problems?"

Nula forced herself to turn away from the remarkable vista of stars and smiled at Zada. "Professor Taguna brought it up during one of his lectures. My brother has been sitting in on his presentations for years. Your son went to every one of his speeches and we listened through the glow star."

Zada nodded his head. "Of course," he said. "That explains a lot."

Squawking over the intercom startled both of them. "Permission to—" they heard Panova bellow, but the door to the bridge opened before he could finish his request.

"You're already programed for access," Nula yelled over to him and waved for him to join her.

Panova had to bend considerably to avoid hitting his head on the door frame. Most of ceilings aboard *Rescue One* were at least ten feet high, which gave the giant two and half feet of head room, but the doorway openings were only six feet eight inches. He was wearing new pants and a new shirt. His boots were scratched and scuffed, but at least he had on new socks. Nula watched him intently. "What a handsome man. You look very nice," she said, standing to greet him. "Bend down, you big gorgeous hulk, so I can give you a kiss."

Panova smiled, picked her up and kissed her. "Isn't this better than punching me?"

"You remember that?" Nula said hugging his left arm.

Panova looked down at Nula. "Of course, I do. You're the only one in the universe who was ever brave enough to hit me." They burst into laughter.

He set her down and stood at attention in front of Zada. "My sir."

"Stand down," Zada ordered, inviting Panova to join them at the table.

Dauntless entered the bridge, a stack of papers in his arms. Stone was beside him.

Hearing the hilarity, Stone yelled over. "What are we missing?"

Nula ran over and threw her arms around him. "We're just having fun."

Dauntless acknowledged Zada, placed the stack of papers

on the table and then turned to Panova. "Congratulations, First Officer Panova. Welcome to the crew of *Rescue One*." Dauntless held out his hand and then realized that Panova had no idea what the gesture meant. He grabbed his hand and shook it.

The giant bowed. "I am honored. I am not sure what the duties of a first officer are but I will always give you my total allegiance."

Nula moved next to Panova and love-punched him on the wrist because she couldn't reach his shoulder. "Keep recruiting our crew," she said. She looked at Stone and winked. "We have one hundred eight new crew, Captain."

After the pleasantries were over, they all sat quietly at the table. Everyone was looking at Zada and waiting for him to speak. He remained silent, collecting his thoughts. Nula looked at her brother and then at Stone, thinking that they looked too serious.

She punched her brother. "You didn't tell Panova how nice his new clothes look. Remember laughing at me when I suggested we put the weaving machines aboard?" She stared at Dauntless. "Go ahead tell him how nice he looks."

Stone picked up on her ploy to lighten the mood. "Ya, tell him how nice he looks," he prodded.

Dauntless chuckled.

Zada cleared his throat, leaned back in his chair. "I had a long conversation with Chalot, the alliance's director of operations. She acknowledges the great work you've done at the surveillance module and on Miranda. The entire alliance expresses its gratitude for your bravery and determination. You have saved thousands of lives. Your selflessness has earned their respect and admiration." He lowered his eyes and gazed at the table in silence.

Dauntless reached over and placed his hand on top of the stack of papers he had brought with him. "They are going to board us when we arrive at Marsha, aren't they?" he asked.

"Yes," Zada answered. "Everyone is extremely concerned how two young Earthlings could achieve such extraordinary achievements in such a short time."

Dauntless patted the stack of papers. He spoke quietly. "Everything the glow star has created is right here. We have nothing to hide. I will instruct Prodigy to expose his files to whomever the alliance authorizes."

Zada softened his gaze. "Thank you." He took in a deep breath and exhaled, still staring into Dauntless's eyes trying to find the slightest glimpse of pride or arrogance. What he identified was calm, peace and purity. "Ah, the glow star," he continued. "You must understand that the search to unlock its secrets extends over a thousand years. Billions of our population have failed." He reached over and touched Dauntless's and Nula's hands. "And what do I do?" He sighed. "I give it to an Earthling from a restricted planet, who uses it to create the most sophisticated technology the universe has ever known."

Nula placed her other hand over Zada's and looked deep into his eyes. "Isn't that wonderful?" she said.

"What do you mean?" Zada asked, mesmerized by her loveliness. *Nula the goddess of beauty,* flashed through his mind.

Nula smiled. "The glow star can only be used for the good of humanity. Ergo, its creations must be virtuoso." She stood up and placed her open palms flat against the table. "Anyhow," she continued, "I had an epiphany while laying suspended in the operating room with the power of the glow star drenching over me. If any of its creations were ever to be used for evil, they would vanish." She moved to where Stone was seated, stood behind him and wrapped her arms around his neck. "Let's go to Marsha so I can meet your mom. Then go find your spaceship." She turned and headed towards the flight chairs.

Dauntless rushed to catch up to her. When he was close, he whispered in her ear. "I talked to Dad earlier. He said they are two years ahead of schedule on *Rescue Two*.

The end

About *Rescue One*

Over the years, I have been scribbling notes about great space discoveries and innovating advancements in technology, some a reality, others in various stages of development. I thought it would be fun to mention a few.

Facts about *Rescue One* revealed in this story and in stories to come:

- Glow Star (Energy Sphere): given to Kevin in the book *Billbet's Space Adventure*. It was a gift from Billbet's (Stone's) dad, Zada, to show his appreciation for helping his son get back to his home planet, Usra. The person in possession of the glow star has the capability to create whatever they can imagine but only if they are pure of heart. It will only respond if the user's intentions will benefit the population of the universe.
- Prodigy: a self-learning singularity super quantum computer.
- Bee's (PBs Prodigy Bees): flying robots that are programmed to an individual's DNA and become that person's direct connection to Prodigy. They also are equipped with a powerful laser.
- Bee's Laser: capable of scanning DNA and then attacking that DNA to disable all motor skills. Can be used to cut through steel or melt metal alloys.
- Atomic Diamond Batteries: diamonds that are

encapsulated with atomic waste to generate power. Battery life is thirty-four thousand years.

• Robot Cubes: modular building compartments that will become the *Rescue One* space station. Each modular is fully equipped and functional. The cubes are programmed and once in space they will be deployed and locked into place to become the *Rescue One*.

• *Rescue One* Space Station: three hundred ninety meters long, fifteen stories high and two hundred twenty meters wide. All food is grown in the greenhouses. Fresh water is captured and stored from passing asteroids or can be made in the distillery. There are a number of smaller landing craft and cargo ships aboard in various sizes that can be used as shuttles. There are forty launch and capture bays. It is totally self-sufficient and can remain in space indefinitely. It is beyond state-of-the-art technology that was developed with the assistance of the glow star. The three-dimensional printers are capable of creating any item that is aboard the station and can be programed for additional needs. The space ship travels through dimensional speed and is undetectable while in vibrating strings.

• Quantum Particle Entanglement Reactor: a transportation method to traverse the universe. By combining three new revelations from the glow star (super speed laser, vibrating strings and the quantum particle entanglement) it is possible to choose two locations irrelevant to distance and instantly bring the two locations together. Prodigy's precise universe coordinates (given to Dauntless by Stone) will cause the entanglement to be activated in the desired direction and allow for modifications to the exact distance from the desired particle.

- Plasma Rocket Thrusters: uses electrical fields to heat gases millions of degrees hotter than a traditional engine. Can thrust the craft three times faster than a traditional engine. Used for short distances, less than one hundred thousand miles.
- Steller Engine (In development stages): could move the entire solar system. The thruster would sit close to one of the Sun's poles and use electromagnetic fields to gather hydrogen and helium from the solar wind to use as fuel that would power two jets of energy, one using helium pushed through a fusion reactor to create a jet of radioactive oxygen that would move the thrusters forward. The other jet would use hydrogen to maintain distance from the Sun and push it forward. The thruster is a giant, curved mirror designed to reflect enough of the photons in the sun's radiation.
- Mechanical Medical Spiders: microscopic robots injected in the body. They diagnosis and heal many afflictions.
- Robot Sled: used to transport materials and personnel from deep space to *Rescue One.*.
- Robot Stretchers: used to transport patients aboard *Rescue One.*
- Drones: unmanned, or two and four passengers.
- Spherical and Rectangular Coordinate Identification System: used to program vibrating strings to particle entanglement.
- Clone Machines: used to clone needed body parts. They can also clone needed food supplies such as fish, chicken, beef, etc.
- Three-dimensional printers: used to create needed spare parts.
- Pain Jelly: used during operations and for injured body

parts.

- Pain Gas: used in conjunction with operating sealed environment compartments.
- Tracer Tags: injected into the body by needle. Can be tracked in deep space or while on planets.
- Ray Machine: replaces X-ray and all other scanning devices. Patient suspended in a gaseous state allows total imaging of the entire body internally as well as externally.
- Ear Node Translator: allows the translation of all languages. Tied to Stone's computer and eventually to Prodigy.
- Black Matter Sound Canon: defensive weapon. Sound blast created from black matter energy, which disorients an individual, reduces cognitive abilities and creates a loss of motor skills.
- Stun Ray: a billion candle watts temporarily blinds individual into submission.
- Dissolving Restraints: used to protect extremely injured individuals who cannot control their own movements. Also used on detained individuals. They unlock once the person calms down.
- Electro Energy Blast: can disable any electronic devices.
- Indestructible Rope: cannot be severed by sharp objects. It can only be cut using a molecule laser.
- Molecule Laser: used to sever indestructible rope.
- Energy Needle: extends out one hundred feet in front of *Rescue One* while it's in dimensional travel. It gathers and stores energy created from friction and black matter.

Also by Frank Gratton

Billbet's Space Adventure